A
Harlequin
Romance

HEIR TO GLEN GHYLL

by

LUCY GILLEN

HARLEQUIN BOOKS

Winnipeg • Canada   New York • New York

HEIR TO GLEN GHYLL

First published in 1970 by Mills & Boon Limited,
17 - 19 Foley Street, London, England.

Harlequin Canadian edition published December, 1970
Harlequin U.S. edition published March, 1971

Standard Book Number: 373-51450-6.

Printed in Canada

CHAPTER ONE

THE long, quiet and not very smooth road seemed endless to Mora, although the country they were driving through was breathtakingly impressive and she gazed out at it enchanted. Distant blue hills appeared mistily in the haze of early winter and the varying greens of turf and heather made settings for the wide sweeping expanses of water that varied in colour from deep, dark blue to glowering grey. Outcrops of rock broke the shallow edges and ruffled the wind stirred water into white frills of movement.

It was everything she had expected and more, but she found her mind frequently wandering from the beauties around her to other more personal and less soothing matters. The thought uppermost in her mind at the moment was one which had been with her all the way from London —whether she had been too impulsive in accepting Hamish's invitation to come home with him to Glen Ghyll, and meet his family. Not that she anticipated anything unpleasant would happen, but it had all been arranged in rather a hurry and she wished she had taken more time to think. Time to realise that perhaps the family she was to meet would interpret the reason for her visit as a much more personal one than was true at the moment.

She glanced at the man beside her in the driving seat of the car, whose dark face was stern now in concentration, as if his thoughts too, were elsewhere. It seemed such a long time since she had first met Hamish McLean, but in fact it was only a little over four months ago, at the opening of a new art gallery. They had taken an instant liking to one another and Mora's claim to descent from the same branch

5

of the McLeans to which he belonged had formed an immediate bond, so that they had spent most of the time talking about their mutual ancestry. She told him she was writing a history of the McLeans and Hamish had offered all the help he could, and been delighted to.

He was not a man who made friends easily, he admitted that, but he had been immediately attracted to Mora, not least because she was a very lovely girl, and the family history had proved an excellent reason for furthering their acquaintance. He had found her very easy to talk to and noticed the many envious glances in his direction during the afternoon, for Mora was a girl that men noticed no matter how absorbed they might be in traditional art.

Her heart-shaped face had a loveliness that stemmed as much from an inner warmth as from any physical perfection. Dark brown hair, not quite black, curled softly about her face and her dark blue eyes were fringed with long thick lashes, a legacy from an Irish father.

Hamish counted himself lucky to have met her, and from then on they had met frequently and talked incessantly, about Glen Ghyll and the history of the family. Lately, however, Mora had noticed a much more personal tone in their conversations, and two weeks ago Hamish had declared himself in love with her. The admission had not altogether surprised her, but she wished he had not made it, or at least that he had waited for a while until she was more certain of her feelings.

She was very fond of Hamish, it was difficult not to be, for he had a quiet charm and an air of sincerity that she found very attractive, and he treated her with a courtesy that was almost old world and very flattering. Added to that he was quite good-looking, although perhaps a little too rugged for conventional handsomeness.

His hair was almost as dark as her own and thick as a thatch above the broad brow and grey eyes, while his straight nose and mouth had an uncompromising look that spoke of stubbornness and perhaps temper, although she

6

had never seen him lose his temper in the months she had known him.

The invitation to join him on the journey north had come as something of a surprise and she had accepted it almost without stopping to consider what the reason behind it had been. He was returning home, he told her, and might not be back in London for perhaps a year or even longer. His business was completed and he was leaving for Glen Ghyll in three days' time. If she would come with him she could not only meet the rest of his family as he wanted her to, but also gather more material for her book at first hand.

The question of there being accommodation for her he laughed to scorn, for Glen Ghyll had ample room to take a whole regiment if necessary. It had been the thought of actually staying in the castle that had decided her, though she had not admitted as much to Hamish.

The prospect of really seeing the castle, somewhere that, until now, had existed only in vague tales handed down from her grandfather, thrilled her and she had perhaps not given her answer as much thought as she should have done. However, it was too late now and she would simply have to let it be known from the start of her visit that she was to be there purely to help her research for her book.

'Nearly there.' His voice, breaking the silence, startled her for a moment so that she turned her head sharply to look at him and saw him smile. 'You've been deep in thought for the last couple of miles,' he said. 'You're not having second thoughts, are you, Mora?'

She shook her head. 'No, of course I'm not.' Her answer was not quite truthful, but she hoped he would not suspect it. 'Why should I have second thoughts?' She arched a curious brow, her smile half teasing. 'There isn't some dark family secret you haven't told me about, is there?'

'Secret?' He seemed to take her question seriously despite the accompanying smile.

'I was only joking, Hamish.' She put a hand to touch his arm briefly and felt the muscles in it tense under her fingers. 'I'm nervous, to be perfectly frank,' she confessed. 'It's quite an ordeal for me, you know, meeting the McLeans, and in such grand surroundings too, though I must admit I'm looking forward to seeing the castle. I've heard so much about it from my mother. My grandfather lived there for a while as a boy.'

He glanced at her as they turned off the road they had been following and on to a narrower and much rougher one. 'I don't see that you have anything to be nervous about,' he said. 'We're just an ordinary family.'

She laughed her disbelief at the opinion. 'Hardly ordinary,' she denied. 'Not every family lives in a castle and owns half the countryside around them.'

'Well, perhaps not ordinary in that way,' he allowed. 'We've lived at Glen Ghyll a long time and we've managed to retain most of what we started out with *and* more, but we're ordinary people as far as we ourselves are concerned. Besides,' he reminded her, 'it's your own family in a way, isn't it? After all, you *are* a McLean.'

Mora laughed, her eyes on a glimpse of mellow grey stone seen through a maze of bare tree branches about two hundred yards ahead. 'I hardly think that having a McLean for a maternal grandfather gives me the right to call myself family,' she said. 'But it's sweet of you to try and make me feel at home, Hamish, and I appreciate it.'

'I hope it *will* be your home,' he told her quietly, and she frowned briefly. 'Oh, I know,' he added hastily, 'you'd rather I didn't talk about the way I feel—about my feelings for you, but I have to admit here and now that I'm hoping a stay at Glen Ghyll and being with me in my own environment will help you to see me differently. Help you to make up your mind about me.' She made no answer and sensed his disappointment. 'I shall have to spend some time in Cairndale, of course, and there will be meetings and such with the rest of the family, but I'm not tied to business all the time, and there's so much I can show you.'

'I know,' she said softly. 'And I shall enjoy being here

8

enormously, Hamish, I know I shall.'

A smile flicked across his dark face as he turned his head and looked at her. 'You'll be quite the loveliest woman the old place has ever seen,' he told her gallantly and with the sincerity she had come to expect of him, and she smiled her thanks as they neared the end of their journey.

The narrow little road meandered on into the distance, but Hamish turned the car into a wide, well-kept driveway that ran between tall trees, stripped and gaunt now with the coming winter, but still thick and close enough to give the impression of a guard lining the approach to the castle.

At the end of the drive the castle itself loomed magnificently, with an arched gateway offering access to a rectangular courtyard. Passing through the gateway Mora had a second's glimpse of someone standing in the shadows under the ancient stones, well back to allow the car to pass, and she had a fleeting impression of glittering eyes and a dark face, too brief to recognise features or even to be sure that she had really seen anyone at all, and for one idiotic moment she wondered if it had been a real man or merely a shade from the castle's long history.

If Hamish noticed anything, he made no sign that he had, but drove straight on round the courtyard to pull up before a pair of massive dark wood doors, one of which stood slightly ajar. Closed in by its massive walls the castle looked even more impressive than it had from the road, in those glimpses between the trees. It was solid-looking and huge and less friendly than she had hoped, but perhaps it was the darkness of the winter day that made it look as if its many windows glowered at her disapprovingly from the four sides of the courtyard.

Hamish left his seat and hastened round to open the car door for her, his hand firm and reassuring under her elbow as they went up the two steps to the doors. As if on cue, the door already ajar opened wider and a woman stood back to allow them to enter, a smile of welcome on her face for Hamish.

9

'Mr. Hamish!' She clasped her plump hands together in front of her, her small bright eyes beaming her pleasure and Hamish put his hands on her arms and embraced her briefly before turning back to Mora.

'Mora, I'd like you to meet a very important person in my young life—Miss Jeannie McKenzie, Nana to us. She's been at Glen Ghyll most of her life.' He smiled down at Mora with a proprietorial air that did not altogether please her. 'Nana, this is our guest, Miss O'Connell. Miss Mora O'Connell.'

The little round face of the woman wrinkled into another welcoming smile as she took both Mora's hands in hers. 'Miss O'Connell.' The neatly coiffured white head tilted to one side as she studied Mora and it was all too obvious what thoughts were passing through her mind. 'A bonny young lady, Mr. Hamish,' she opined softly, her eyes glistening with pleasure. 'Aye, real bonny.' She smiled at them both benevolently, approving Hamish's choice, and Mora tried not to mind too much. Already the wrong idea had been firmly planted in one mind and she doubted it would be easy to convince the old lady of her mistake.

'You look fine,' Hamish told her, as if he sensed Mora's dislike of the automatic assumption; Nana nodded.

'Aye, I'm fine,' she said. 'But come away in now, you'll catch your death standing there in that cold doorway. Come away in.' She moved behind them and closed the heavy door with a thud that somehow sounded ominous to Mora, though she realised she was being fanciful. The soft Highland accent as the old lady chattered away did something to ease Mora's nervousness and she looked around her with interest. 'Everyone's in the big room,' the old lady informed Hamish, 'and they'll not have heard you come or they'd have been out to meet you, surely.'

The vast hall, Mora decided, could have been taken straight from a film or stage set, it was so perfect and so exactly as she had pictured it. The floor was stone but thickly carpeted for warmth and the walls, dark-panelled part way, swept upwards for an incredible height and displayed antique shields and weapons, everything bearing the dull gleam of good care. A little right of centre a staircase led up to the next floor and such a staircase as Mora had never seen in reality before. The treads were quite shallow, wide and well worn with the dark wood uncarpeted and glowing richly in the light from a large window, half-way up, so that even in the gloom of winter it looked immensely grand.

Mora gazed at it in fascination, deciding that it would take very little imagination, on her part, to visualise the many ancestors who had trodden that stairway in the past four hundred years and left their mark on the history of Glen Ghyll.

'The family,' Hamish informed her, catching the direction of her gaze and mistaking its target. Portraits of varying size covered the walls on both sides of the stairs and continued on to the part of a landing that she could see. 'There are three hundred years of McLeans there,' he told her. 'You must meet them later on; in the meantime you'll have to be content with the present two generations.'

The reminder brought her back to reality and she hastily smoothed down her coat and touched a nervous hand to her hair as Jeannie McKenzie opened a door and the sound of voices reached her. It had been referred to as the big room, and it was no misnomer, for Mora was momentarily overwhelmed by it.

It might have been a banqueting hall in the old days, and indeed a long dark Jacobean table stood against one wall as a reminder, though the room was furnished now more as a sitting room. A profusion of armchairs, divans and occasional tables scattered about it were all but lost in the vast space, but for all its size the room had a welcome warmth which was due only in part to the huge open fire at one side and it looked cosy and inviting as they followed the little woman in.

In a first hasty glance round the room, Mora counted five

11

people. One, a man, stood beside the huge fireplace looking every inch the master of all he surveyed, and Mora recognised him as Sir James McLean, Member of Parliament for several years and head of the thriving family concern that gave the McLeans their enormous wealth. He had earned the reputation, in Parliament, for plain speaking, and seeing him now, feet planted firmly apart, sharp-eyed and alert, Mora could well believe it.

At their entrance he put down the glass he had been drinking from and came forward in great strides, a smile of welcome on his broad face, grasping Hamish's hand as he spoke.

'Hamish! Welcome back, welcome back!' A pair of startlingly blue eyes turned on Mora as she stood, a little behind Hamish, and a second later a vast hand engulfed hers and shook it until her fingers numbed. 'And you'll be Mora O'Connell, eh?' The piercing eyes swept her from head to toe and obviously approved of what they saw.

'Yes, Father, this is Mora.' Hamish sounded very formal after his father's exuberant welcome. 'Mora, this is my father.'

Mora had barely time to murmur a conventional greeting before the great voice boomed out again. 'Lovely girl, lovely girl. You say you're related to the McLeans, Miss O'Connell? Hamish told me about your book, very interesting.'

Mora smiled, somewhat overwhelmed. 'My maternal grandfather was a McLean, Sir James, Robert McLean. He came from here—from Glen Isla, actually, but he spent time here as a child.'

'Oh, *that* Robert McLean.' The bright eyes surveyed her again, this time with a more shrewd interest. 'I know about him, of course, from my father. Robert McLean was a cousin of my grandfather and he eloped with a girl my grandfather was to marry. Caused a bit of a stir at the time, I believe. They went to England or Ireland, I forget which, but my father used to mention it on occasion.' He frowned

12

his curiosity suddenly. 'If you're Robert McLean's grand-daughter,' he stated bluntly, 'you're very young. If he's still alive he must be over ninety, and you and I are scarcely contemporary, are we?'

Mora flushed at having her ancestry doubted; however she managed to smile. 'He would be about that if he was still alive,' she said. 'I never knew him. My mother looked after him for nearly thirty years after my grandmother died and it was only after he died that she married.'

'Ah, I see; that accounts for the generation gap.' The broad face beamed another smile at her, as if he guessed something of her nervousness. 'We tend to marry young in our branch of the family,' he told her. 'Though only Fergus has followed tradition so far.' Fergus, Mora knew, was Hamish's younger brother.

As if he feared his father might say too much on the subject of his own marrying, Hamish took her arm and they crossed the room to enter a circle of curious eyes. 'Come and meet the rest of the family,' he said, while Sir James followed their progress with his bright intent gaze, as if he would have liked to know more of his son's plans regarding Mora.

Another, very slightly younger version of Hamish rose from a chair near the fire and proffered a hand, smiling at her in the same friendly but slightly reserved way that Hamish had at their first meeting. 'My brother, Fergus,' Hamish told her, and himself shook hands with his brother.

'You're welcome, Miss O'Connell,' Fergus told her. 'I hope you'll like Glen Ghyll.'

'I'm sure I will,' Mora smiled. 'It's very impressive and I'm sure I shall find a lot that's very useful for my book.' She thought she detected a puzzled look in his eyes at her deliberate allusion to why she was there, and he glanced at his brother enquiringly.

'Mora's writing a family history,' Hamish enlightened him. 'She's hoping to delve into our dim and distant past while she's here.'

'Oh, I see.' Fergus McLean, she thought, looked slightly uneasy at the news, and she wondered why.

Nearby, in one of the armchairs, sat a tall gauche-looking girl with a bundle of knitting in her lap and she looked up with a shy half smile when they approached. 'Fergus's wife, Tricia,' Hamish said, an edge of impatience on his voice as the girl fumbled for a moment at the mound of knitting with her long fingers, then dropped it in a tangled mass on to her knees while she shook hands. She looked at her brother-in-law apologetically and Mora felt a twinge of pity for her.

'Hello,' the girl said breathlessly, reaching to retrieve a ball of wool that threatened to escape under a chair.

Mora picked it up for her before either of the two men could move, and handed it back with a smile, wondering how soon Sir James was to be a grandfather. Hamish bent and administered a brotherly peck on her cheek. 'We call her Tizzy,' he explained to Mora dryly, 'because she's usually in one.'

'And don't you mind?' Mora asked her with a smile. 'It seems rather unkind.'

'Oh, I don't mind in the least,' Tricia McLean said, still in that breathless voice that betrayed her nervousness. 'Actually Fergus christened me that when I first knew him and the rest of the family have adopted it since.' Wide and almost childlike blue eyes looked up at her. 'You're welcome to call me Tizzy as well if you like, everyone else does.'

Mora smiled her thanks for the privilege. 'I will if you're sure you don't mind,' she said. She would have liked to stay and talk to Tricia McLean longer, but Hamish put a hand under her arm and urged her towards where another woman sat—an older woman this time and ruddy-faced, with bright blue eyes that betrayed her relationship to Sir James.

'My aunt, Miss Alison McLean,' Hamish said, and bent to kiss the woman's cheek as she shook hands with Mora. 'It's nice to see you again, Aunt Alison, how are you?'

14

'Fit, as always,' his aunt replied crisply, and turned her shrewd eyes on Mora. 'Glad to see a girl with roses in her cheeks,' she told her. 'It shows you don't spend your time in those ghastly clubs and things.'

'I am pretty fit,' Mora admitted, finding her a little overwhelmingly hearty. 'I walk quite a bit when I can.'

'Good.' The neat dark head nodded approval. 'Glad to hear it.'

Hamish smiled indulgently at his aunt and turned to the fifth member of the group, his face going blank with surprise when he looked at her, as if he only now realised her identity. 'Hello, Helen, how are you?'

The girl stood beside one of the high windows, so that the light fell on to her face and revealed the perfect complexion and rather fine eyes. It was a face less than pretty but with a certain strange attraction of its own.

'Hello, Hamish, it's nice to see you home again.' There was a little of the same soft accent in her voice that had been evident in the old woman's who had greeted them. Obviously Hamish found her presence there not only unexpected but disconcerting and he looked at her uneasily for a moment or two before remembering his manners.

'Mora.' He put an arm round her shoulders, as if contact with her gave him some sort of courage. 'I'd like you to meet Helen Murdoe, an old—an old friend of the family. Helen, this is Mora O'Connell who's staying with us for a while.'

'Hello, Miss O'Connell.' The smile was friendly enough, but the fine dark eyes had a shrewd look in them, as if she had her own ideas why Mora was there and did not approve of them at all. 'Is this your first visit to Scotland?'

'It is,' Mora admitted, 'and I'm looking forward to it immensely.'

'You're from London?'

Mora nodded. 'Yes, and I think I shall find it very different here. The country we came through looked magnificent, I can't wait to see it at closer quarters.'

The other girl smiled, a smile that Mora found oddly disturbing, though she could think of no reason why she should. 'It's a pity you don't ride, that's by far the best way to see the country round here, but no doubt Hamish will run you round in the car.'

'Oh, but I do ride,' Mora told her with a smile, and saw the other girl frown as if the news displeased her. 'I'm hoping Hamish will act as guide, but if he's busy I'm sure I could find my own way around gradually.'

'Rob Smith, the stable lad, is a good guide if you need one,' Helen Murdoe told her. 'He's a mine of local information.'

'There's no need for Rob Smith,' Hamish interposed hastily, a frown betraying his dislike of the suggestion. 'I'll take you, Mora. In fact we'll start tomorrow morning if you'd like to. We shall have to make the most of the weather before it gets too bad.'

'That sounds like a wonderful idea,' Mora smiled, 'if you're sure you won't be too busy. It seems ages since I rode and I shall have to take it easy for a while, but I'll be ready to start tomorrow morning or any time you say, Hamish. The sooner the better so that I can get the atmosphere of the place.' She saw the enquiring glance that Helen Murdoe flicked at Hamish and the frown of annoyance that drew her dark brows into a straight line across her forehead, while Hamish explained again Mora's reason for staying at Glen Ghyll.

Whatever welcome the McLean family might have extended her, she was certain that Helen Murdoe did not share their pleasure and she wondered what had been, or perhaps still was, between the other girl and Hamish. Whatever it was it had not made Hamish any more glad to see her.

CHAPTER TWO

THE sharpness of late autumn promised a good day when Mora made her way down to breakfast next morning, though it could change very rapidly, she realised. She found the small breakfast room and was once again delighted with what she saw. Once part of the huge kitchens, it was white-walled and invitingly warm, with a big fire burning in the old-fashioned fireplace.

Hamish and his brother, Fergus, were in sole occupation when she came into the room and they both greeted her with smiles uncannily alike, while Hamish drew out a chair for her, managing to brush a caressing hand against her cheek as he seated her.

'Did you sleep well?' he asked, and she nodded, smiling when she remembered the huge dark-panelled room she had been allocated. It had reminded her of every ghost story she had ever read and she had found it so fascinating that she had spent the first half hour of her occupation exploring its possibilities.

'I slept marvellously, thank you,' she said. 'If you have a ghost in that wonderful bedroom I was given, I didn't see or hear him, I'm afraid.'

'There isn't one as far as I know,' Fergus told her with a glance at his brother which he appeared not to notice. 'Is there, Hamish?'

'Not unless you count Adam McLean,' Hamish said with a laugh, 'and he only appears in the north tower on special occasions.' He glanced up and caught his brother's eye at last and hastily amended his account. 'That is,' he added, 'if you believe in such things.'

'Tell me more,' Mora said, looking interested, not less so because she had not missed the warning glance from Fergus and the hasty realisation of Hamish. 'Is Adam McLean among those portraits I passed on the staircase and along the corridor?'

'Yes, he is,' Hamish admitted. 'But we're not very proud of the family villain and don't talk about him.'

'Oh, but you must!' Mora protested with a laugh. 'How villainous was he? I'm sure I haven't come across *him* yet in my research. What did he do?'

'He betrayed his brother to the English,' Hamish told her with as much disapproval in his voice as if the event had been but yesterday, and she had the feeling that he already regretted having mentioned the subject. 'He was a real bad lot.'

'He sounds very intriguing,' said Mora, determinedly pursuing the subject despite opposition. 'I'd love to hear all about him. Why did he betray his brother? Had he a good reason?'

'*Is* there a good reason?' Fergus asked, as if he found her question unanswerable, and Mora felt herself on delicate ground, but Adam McLean was much too interesting a prospect to discard so soon.

She nodded thoughtfully, considering the situation. 'There might be,' she said. 'What was *his* reason?'

Hamish laughed shortly. 'Hardly a *good* reason,' he declared. 'He wanted his brother's wife, you see, so he betrayed him and watched him killed.'

'Ugh! Nasty!' Mora pulled a face. 'I'd like see his portrait, though, he'd make very interesting reading.'

'If you say so,' Hamish said, not very enthusiastically. 'I'll show you after breakfast, only don't be——' He did not finish the sentence, for the door behind him opened to admit his sister-in-law.

She smiled shyly at Mora and walked round the table to sit beside her husband. 'I'm famished,' she announced, her gaunt-looking face appearing even paler this morning. Fer-

18

gus dutifully seated her with a smile on his face that was at once rueful and indulgent. 'I'm ashamed to say I'm always ready for my breakfast.'

'You're always famished,' Fergus told her wryly. 'I never saw such an appetite as you have, my love.'

Tricia McLean giggled like a schoolgirl as he took a plate and filled it for her from the dishes on the sideboard. 'It's the air,' she said. 'It seems more invigorating here than at Glen Isla and it gives me the most enormous appetite.' She looked across at Mora in her shy, half-wary way, as if she sought her support. 'I hope you like your food too, Mora, then I won't feel so greedy.'

'I do,' Mora agreed with a smile. 'And I must admit that the air here does make one extra hungry. I've noticed it already and I've only been here less than twenty-four hours.'

'I've been here nearly a month,' Tricia said ruefully, 'and I've eaten like a horse ever since the first day we came.'

'Oh, I see. You don't always live here?' Mora hoped she did not sound too inquisitive. 'I didn't realise that.'

'We live in the house at Glen Isla,' Tricia explained, and there was a wistfulness about her smile that told its own story. 'But it's this grandchild, you see. Father McLean wanted him born at Glen Ghyll.' She laughed softly, her gaunt face almost pretty as she flushed rosily. 'If it *is* a boy, of course.'

'It will be,' Fergus told her confidently, and Tricia smiled as he put a well-filled plate before her. 'The McLean firstborn is always a boy.'

His wife pulled a wry face at Mora across the table. 'I shall feel as if I've let everybody down very badly if it's a girl,' she said. 'There's so much history and tradition attached to Glen Ghyll, isn't there? Are you doing what they call research, Mora? Is that what you call it? It's very intriguing, isn't it? Writing about the family, I mean, there's such a tremendous lot to learn about. All those hundreds of years.'

'I'm looking forward to it,' said Mora, and glanced at Hamish. 'When I've eaten, I'll hold you to that promise to show me the family villain in the portrait gallery, Hamish.'

Tricia looked interested. 'You mean the other Adam?' she asked, and Mora was aware of a brief, telling silence before Hamish answered her.

'Adam McLean,' he said, 'our black sheep. Mora thinks he'd make interesting reading in her book.'

'Oh, I'm sure he would,' Tricia agreed enthusiastically. 'He must have been a very attractive villain judging by his portrait. No wonder his brother's wife found him irresistible and fell in love with him.'

Mora looked interested. 'Did she? I didn't hear that part.'

Tricia laughed. 'Oh yes, indeed she did. By all accounts she was no better than Adam McLean as far as poor old Robert was concerned.'

'You mean she was in the plot to betray her husband and have him killed?' Mora asked, and Tricia nodded, seeming not to notice the expressions of the two brothers as they ate their breakfasts in silence.

'She was,' said Tricia. 'But you wait until you see him, you'll know what I mean. Bloody Adam they call him, and the family aren't very proud of him at all, but he was certainly very attractive. To look at, anyway. Funny,' she added thoughtfully, 'how like his current namesake he is.'

Mora looked around at the faces of the three of them—Tricia with her bland unawareness of having caused the frowns of uneasiness on the faces of her husband and his brother. There followed a silence which Mora hesitated to break and it was Hamish, opening a complete change of subject, who eventually spoke.

'Right after breakfast I have to see Father about some business that won't wait, Mora, but we can go for that ride as soon as you like after that.' Mora, from the corner of her eyes, saw Fergus gently put a hand on his wife's arm and discreetly shake his head.

'After I've seen the portraits,' Mora insisted, braving another frown. 'I can look round them while you talk to Sir James, Hamish, I don't mind. I can browse on my own for as long as you like.'

The idea apparently suited him better than being called upon to point out his notorious ancestor and perhaps answer Mora's inevitable question about a modern namesake, a point which she admitted was intriguing her. He nodded agreement. 'If you'd like to,' he said. 'There are plenty of them to keep you occupied for quite a while.'

It was rather a pity, Mora thought, as she studied the collection of past McLeans later, that some of the earlier occupants of the castle had not been portrayed—the real old chieftains who had built the first castle and defended it against all comers. However, those who had been committed to canvas over the last three hundred years or so were impressive enough.

They were rugged rather than handsome men and their women sometimes quite lovely, in the oddly blank way of old paintings. She paused before one picture of a young woman, perhaps her own age, but with sandy red hair and rather sly-looking eyes that seemed to issue a challenge to the viewer.

Fashionably dressed in the style of her period, in a drab dark green that served to show her red hair and creamy skin to advantage, she was not a pretty woman, but there was a strange magnetism about her that came across even on paint and canvas and down nearly two and a half centuries.

The date, on a small plaque beneath the painting, was given as 1741 and the name as Marjorie Stewart McLean, wife of Robert McLean. Mora studied her for a while, finding her strangely fascinating, and wondering at the same time why the date should strike her as significant. She moved away after a while to look at the neighbouring portrait, which was of a man, brown-haired and rather dull-looking and presumably the husband of the sandy-haired

Marjorie, since the date given was again 1741 and the name of the sitter, Robert McLean. Tricia had referred to the wronged husband in the story of Adam McLean's villainy, as 'poor old Robert', she remembered, and took a further interest in the oddly matched couple, side by side above that grand staircase down which they must often have passed.

Curiously she studied them both, remembering Adam McLean's crime of betraying his brother to the English, and now it all became clearer. The year 1745 had been the date of the Jacobite uprising and one of the bloodiest episodes in Scottish history. No wonder the family were not exactly proud of their notorious ancestor. Nevertheless she felt the tingle of excitement as she scanned the nearest portraits for Adam McLean. Two of the participants in the gory tale were here; surely somewhere quite close she would find the villain who had betrayed his brother for the sake of acquiring his wife. She glanced again at the sandy-haired woman and her dour-looking husband before moved on, seeking the main character in the drama.

She found Adam McLean several steps removed from the woman he had coveted enough to kill for—a small but exquisitely detailed portrait of a man who must have been, as Tricia claimed, very attractive. Even to modern eyes there was a fascination about the bold face, darker than most of the others and with his own dark hair tied back from a broad forehead. A strong face and insolent in its expression, as if he cared little for the opinion of others, and with deep grey eyes and a stubborn chin, and a trace of a smile round the straight mouth that spoke of humour rather than cruelty.

'Are you admiring the villain of the piece?' a voice asked from just below her on the stairs, and she started almost guiltily out of her reverie to look down at the self-same face that a second before had looked out of the portrait.

The same deep grey eyes glinted mockingly at her as he came up the stairs towards her and for a moment she experienced a chill of panic, staring at him unbelievingly, until she noticed the riding breeches and boots he wore with a roll-necked sweater and realised it was no ghost who had spoken to her, but a living man.

She could, she thought, be forgiven her momentary panic, for the likeness was uncanny and the high collar of the sweater gave much the same impression at first glance as the white stock at the neck of the painted man.

'I've heard about him,' she said uncertainly, an unbidden excitement making her voice tremble. 'I—I wanted to see him.'

He came and stood beside her on the stairs, the strong dark face so like the painting they both faced that she still found it hard to believe. Even the hair was the same thick, dark brown, though cut fairly short except for a piece that fell forward and covered an inch or two of the broad forehead.

Her obvious curiosity seemed to amuse him, for he laughed and shook his head. 'I'm not a ghost,' he assured her, 'but I am his namesake, Adam McLean the second.' He proffered a hand which she took blindly not even noticing that he held it for rather longer than was necessary, while the grey eyes studied her from head to toe, much as Sir James had done the night before.

The other Adam McLean, Tricia McLean had said, and no further explanation had been offered. She prickled with resentment at the bold appraisal and hastily withdrew her captive hand. Whoever he was he was sadly lacking in the gallantry and charm that Hamish possessed. 'I'm Mora O'Connell,' she said, 'a friend of Hamish's.'

'Oh?' Dark brows arched expressively. 'I'd never have given brother Hamish credit for such good taste. When did you arrive?'

'Last night,' Mora answered, her mind spinning dizzily with this new information. She had been under the impression that Fergus was Hamish's only brother. He had never mentioned another in all the time she had known him, and

23

yet this stranger was claiming to be another brother and, judging by the way the subject had been carefully avoided at breakfast, not a very popular one.

As though he guessed something of her thoughts, Adam McLean smiled wryly at her. 'Didn't you know I existed?' he asked. 'Judging by your face, you didn't.'

'I—I thought that Fergus was Hamish's brother—I mean,' she amended hastily, 'his only brother.'

He laughed again, and Mora could imagine the man in the portrait having a laugh just like that, short and insolent, in keeping with the arrogant features and superb self-confidence. 'That's the way they like it,' he informed her, as if it mattered little to him whether his family approved of him or not. 'Actually I'm the black sheep of the brood.' The bold eyes glinted at her in amusement. 'That's why they didn't mention me. Have you met Grandfather yet? Or have they forgotten him, too?'

Mora shook her head, wondering how many more surprises the McLean family had in store for her. 'No, I haven't met him,' she said. 'I met what I thought was the entire family yesterday afternoon. Sir James, your brother Fergus and his wife, Miss Alison McLean and a Miss Murdoe. I—I didn't know there was anyone else.'

The deep eyes glittered wickedly for a moment as he considered the information. 'Helen was here?' Mora nodded, remembering the other's lack of enthusiasm at the news that Mora was to stay for a while at Glen Ghyll. 'Well, well. That must have put the cat among the pigeons.' She thought the slightly crooked smile he wore made him look cruel and she decided, quite definitely, and without hesitation, that she was not going to like Adam McLean, no matter how much he resembled his attractive and rakish ancestor.

'I don't think so,' she said stiffly. 'Everyone behaved normally.'

'Mmm.' He eyed her again, thoughtfully. 'I wonder why they didn't mention you were coming, Tizzy particularly.

24

I'm surprised she didn't let it out if she knew.'

'I—I don't know how many people knew I was coming, it was rather a sudden decision,' said Mora, feeling uncomfortably vulnerable in the company of this arrogant stranger. The family as a whole were rather overwhelming, with the exception of Tricia, and she wondered uneasily how many more of them there were that she had not heard of. 'Is—are there any more of the family I didn't meet?' she asked cautiously, and he looked at her for a moment in silence, then the mocking smile reappeared.

'Well, there's Grandfather McLean,' he informed her. 'The old man stays in his room. He prefers it that way and so does everyone else.' There could have been a trace of bitterness in the last statement. 'I was on my way to see him when I bumped into you.' He eyed her speculatively for a moment. 'Why don't you come with me?' he suggested.

She hesitated, feeling uncharacteristically shy under the challenging gaze. 'Is—is it all right if I do?' she ventured. 'I mean——'

'Of course it's all right,' he interrupted impatiently. 'He won't eat you and neither will I.' He sighed resignedly and ran a hand through his thick hair. 'I hope to heaven Hamish hasn't landed us with another Tizzy who doesn't know whether she's coming or going,' he declared. 'I wouldn't stand it.'

Mora flushed angrily, feeling bound to defend the inoffensive Tricia. 'I found Mrs. McLean very nice,' she said shortly. 'She seems to me to be a very sweet person.'

'Oh, I agree, she is,' he concurred agreeably. 'But poor Tizzy isn't exactly the brightest girl in captivity, you must agree.'

'She *is* your brother's wife,' she pointed out, stiffly disapproving though she sensed his amusement at her manner. 'I don't think you should speak of her in that way to a newcomer.'

The deep eyes glistened with laughter as he looked at her

and she thought he looked more than ever like the portrait facing them. 'You *are* a newcomer or you wouldn't expect conventional drawing-room manners from me,' he told her. 'Now, I'm going up to see the old man, so if you're coming, stop havering, woman, and come.'

Mora flushed to the roots of her hair, her eyes sparkling angrily at his deliberate rudeness. 'I'm *not* coming, Mr. McLean, thank you. I have to see Hamish very shortly and I told him I'd be looking at the portraits. Besides,' she added, glancing at his own attire, 'we're riding and I have to go and change.'

He shrugged, the smile still in evidence, though the glitter in his eyes could have been anger at her refusal to accompany him. 'Suit yourself,' he said. 'I'll see you around some time. By the way,' he paused in his long stride up the rest of the stairs, 'are you staying long?'

'I'm not sure,' Mora demurred.

The grin he gave her over his shoulder made her feel uneasy again as he swept the bold gaze over her again from head to toe. 'I hope so,' he said, 'you could make life very interesting.' He turned round on the step, two or three above her. 'Anyway, why are you here? Are you Hamish's blushing bride or just good friends, as the magazines have it?'

'I'm doing research,' More said chillingly, 'and Hamish said I could stay as long as I liked.' She chose to ignore the question about her relationship with Hamish.

'Research?' The expressive brows flicked upwards again. 'Good grief, you're not some egg-head scientist, are you?'

There really seemed no end to his rudeness, Mora thought angrily, her face betraying her displeasure. 'I'm writing a history of the Glen Ghyll McLeans,' she informed him, and flushed at the laughter in his eyes. 'I'm hoping to learn quite a lot about the family history while I'm here.'

'Oh, you will, Professor, you will,' he assured her with a short laugh. 'Hence your interest in the old Adam, I suppose.'

She juggled with the idea of arguing with him on his manner of addressing her, but she thought it would serve only to worsen her own temper and do little to trouble his, so she merely turned her back on him and went downstairs, forgetting, until she was in the hall again, that she had intended going to her own room to change.

She saw no sign of Adam McLean when she went back upstairs again a few minutes later, and she breathed a sigh of relief. It was to be hoped that he would continue to absent himself from family gatherings as long as she was at Glen Ghyll, though she was curious about him, she had to admit. Curious, too, to know why Hamish had never once mentioned him to her in all the time she had known him. When Tricia had raised the subject it was obvious that it was not a popular one, any more than the first Adam McLean was, though it could scarcely be for the same reason.

The view from her window was breathtaking and she spent so long contemplating it that she was far longer changing than she meant to be and she heard Hamish's voice at her door almost before she was ready. 'I'm sorry I was so long,' she apologised when she joined him. 'I was quite carried away by that view from my window.'

'It *is* lovely, isn't it?' He smiled his pleasure at her praise and took her arm possessively as they walked down the corridor to the stairs. 'We'll go and find some more like it, shall we?'

'Lovely.' She smiled up at him, surreptitiously comparing him with his brother and seeing only a basic family resemblance.

'You're lovely too,' he told her, his grey eyes warm with admiration as he looked down at her from his superior height. 'Very lovely.'

'And you're very flattering,' she replied with a soft laugh, trying to still the flutter her heart gave at the compliment made in his deep, quiet voice. She did not want to become committed to an engagement at the moment, but she could

27

not help feeling charmed and a little excited whenever she was with Hamish. It was going to be difficult being strong-minded enough to resist him being in such close contact with him every day, she could see that, and she sighed inwardly at the prospect. Hamish, she believed, would be gifted with perseverance.

They had reached the top of the stairs when another voice called to them from along the corridor to their left. 'Are you still here?' Adam McLean asked, his mocking eyes on his brother's sudden frown. 'You should know better than to keep a lady waiting this long, Hamish. I nearly ran off with her.'

Mora flushed defensively when she saw Hamish's hasty glance from her to his brother and back again. There was a glint of suspicion in his eyes that she did not like but which Adam McLean seemed to find amusing. 'You know Mora?' he asked, and the other man laughed—the same short, insolent laugh as before, standing with his feet apart, his hands thrust into the pockets of his riding breeches.

'Of course I know Mora,' he said, and challenged Mora to deny it.

'We—we met on the stairs earlier,' Mora hastened to add. 'I was looking at the portrait of your family villain and——'

'And she came face to face with the present one,' Adam McLean interrupted. 'It quite shook her up for a minute, didn't it, Professor?'

'Don't use that silly title,' Mora snapped crossly, and sensed Hamish's surprise, though his brother merely made his usual response and laughed at her.

'Temper, temper,' he warned her. 'I suppose it's having a name like O'Connell. You've got an Irish paddy.'

'Do you have to be so infernally boorish?' Hamish asked coldly, his dark face flushed with suppressed anger. 'What are you doing here, anyway?'

That, Mora decided when she saw the quick frown on Adam McLean's face, did not please him. 'The only thing I ever come to the house for,' he retorted. 'To see Grand-father.'

'Oh yes, of course.' Hamish looked momentarily sheep-ish. 'I must go in and see him myself later on.'

'Do that,' his brother advised wryly, 'and why not take your little Irish Paddy with you? Grandfather likes pretty girls.'

'I will,' Hamish promised, suddenly amenable.

'And you don't have to worry about her, you know,' the other man added with a smile. 'I offered to take her along to see the old man earlier, but she refused to come with me.'

Hamish frowned angrily. 'Which only goes to show she has good sense,' he retorted. 'Shall we go now, Mora? While the weather holds.'

As they turned to go, Mora caught the deep grey eyes watching her, speculative, and arrogant, so that she flushed and hated the betraying colour the more when she heard him laugh softly behind them.

She thought Hamish was more than a little uneasy after the encounter with his brother and decided that this was not an opportune moment to ask him why he had kept his other brother a secret.

A sturdy grey had been saddled for her and stood waiting down on the gravelled sweep of the courtyard before the big doors. Even a morning ride, she thought with a smile, had the air of a grand occasion in such surroundings. A dourly attentive stable lad helped her to mount—the Rob Smith that Helen Murdoe had recommended as a guide.

The grey, she found, was amenable enough to enable her to look around and enjoy the scenery without the need to hold him too hard. It was unusually fine for the time of the year, but a pale wintery sun slanted between grey clouds, promising rain later.

The blue hills swept up on three sides of them, hazy now in the wintery light, but majestic and beautiful with the clouds drifting round them like lacy shawls. The country appeared to be a patchwork of greens and yellows that constantly changed with the light and, like jewels in the setting, the glinting water of one large loch and several small pools. Among them all a narrow stream meandered lazily from one end of the glen to the other.

'It's quite lovely,' Mora opined, as they paused atop the highest piece of ground in the glen. A smoothly rounded mound of stones and earth just large enough to take the two horses side by side.

'It is,' Hamish agreed, and she thought she could imagine his feeling at being back among the tranquillity and silence of this lovely place after so long in the noise and bustle of London. She was nothing loath to stay quiet and enjoy it with him.

There was only the soft jingle of the harness when the horses moved and the sound of the stream over its stony bed, just a few yards away to disturb the silence. It looked, she thought, as if it might have been so tranquil and placidly silent since the beginning of time and yet she knew that it had seen many skirmishes and battles in its long history. The silence must often have been shattered by the cries of men and horses, and, as if they sensed something of the past, their own horses moved restlessly.

'Shall we go?' Hamish asked, and Mora nodded. 'We can go through the burn here and over as far as the loch if you'd like to.'

'I'd love to,' she agreed, but glanced at the tell-tale, slanting rays of the sun on the hillsides. It would not stay fine all day.

The loch was bigger than it had appeared from further away and it looked dark and bottomless as they stood at the edge where the wind ruffled the water against the stones into a necklace of white frills. 'This is Loch Airdren,' Hamish told her. 'There can't have been much rain this year so far, or it would be much more swollen than it is.'

'It looks bottomless,' Mora said, watching the grey water glinting in the pale sunlight, 'and very ominous somehow.'

Hamish laughed. 'I suppose it should look ominous really,' he said. 'It's supposed that the McLeans disposed of their enemies by throwing them into the loch after knocking them unconscious.'

Mora shuddered. 'I'm not sure I altogether approve of our mutual ancestors; they weren't very humane, were they?'

'Oh, I don't know,' Hamish demurred, 'it was quick and merciful, which most deaths weren't in those days. I don't think I'd have minded too much.'

'I suppose not,' she agreed reluctantly. 'But they really were a bloodthirsty lot in those days. By the way,' she added, 'I found the family villain in the gallery and he proved as fascinating as Tizzy said he was. He must have been a very attractive man.' She spoke of the man in the portrait, but her mind persistently recalled his namesake who had introduced himself with much the same arrogance and self-confidence that the other must have possessed.

Hamish frowned as if he found the subject annoying and she wondered if he too was thinking of his brother and not the man in the portrait. 'I'd have given you credit for more sense than Tizzy,' he said bluntly. 'He was a blackguard, and no amount of historical glamour will make him anything else.'

Mora smiled wryly at his opinion, shaking her head slowly. 'You won't convince us, Hamish, however much you try. Women will forgive a man almost anything if he does it for love, whether illicit or not. It's just the way we are.'

He looked at her for a moment uncertainly, then leaned over and covered one of her hands with his own. His grey eyes held a warmth that stirred her uneasily and she lowered her eyes so as not to see it. 'Would you forgive *me* anything, Mora? If I did it for love?' He watched her closely and when she did not answer, he slid from his saddle and came round to the other side of her, his arms upraised. 'Mora?'

Almost unthinkingly she slid down into his arms and a

31

moment later his mouth sought hers, hard and demanding and somehow frightening, so that she stirred in protest and tried to break free. 'Hamish, please!'

'I love you, Mora!' He held her tightly and she looked up into the dark, serious face close above her.

'Give me more time,' she pleaded. 'I have to think about it, Hamish. I asked you to let me have time to get used to the idea.'

'I've known you over four months,' he objected. 'I know how *I* feel, surely you must too.'

'I don't,' she insisted. 'I'm sorry, Hamish, but it's too important a thing to make a hasty decision on. You said, when we came here, that you hoped I would learn to love you in time. Please give me the time you promised me, that's all I ask.'

His grey eyes looked deeper and darker and much more like his brother's as he looked at her. Then he shook his head slowly as if to clear it, his expression part disappointment, part impatience.

'I'm sorry, Mora, I suppose I am trying to rush my fences a bit, but I *do* love you and——' He paused and she wondered if he too was uneasy about his brother Adam and her own reaction to him, though he had no cause to be, heaven knew. If Adam McLean resembled his ancestral namesake physically, that was as far as it went. Her own admiration was reserved solely for the painted version, of that she was quite certain. 'You forgive me?' Hamish's voice broke into her reverie.

She smiled at him. 'Of course, I have to after what I said earlier, don't I? Shall we go before the rain breaks?' she suggested, and turned to remount before her theory on forgiveness was put to the test again.

CHAPTER THREE

MORA wondered, at lunch and at dinner that night, why Adam McLean did not put in an appearance with the rest of the family. Apparently the grandfather spent most of the time in his room, as his grandson had said, and her query about his health had been met with a reluctant admission that he was unable to get about very well. It had been left to Tricia McLean to explain that the old man had had a riding accident several years ago and that he now found movement extremely painful. Consequently he was rather short-tempered as a result.

'Grandfather's all right in his own way,' Fergus said defensively as if he too, as Mora had, detected a note of sympathy in Tricia's voice when she spoke of the old man. 'He wants for nothing and he doesn't enjoy company much, so there's no point in bothering him too often, is there?'

Mora could see the logic of the answer, although it did not seem very much of a life for Grandfather McLean, as they always called him, neither did it explain Adam McLean's absence from the family table, and, much as she regretted it, she found herself curiously interested in him.

'Your brother—Adam goes to see him, doesn't he?' Mora asked, and Fergus looked at her with raised brows as if her question surprised him. Perhaps Hamish had not yet had the opportunity to tell him that Mora had met their other brother, the one they had been so reluctant to acknowledge.

'Adam and Grandfather have always got on together better than the rest of us,' he said, and sounded bitter and resentful, whether he meant to or not.

'You said you'd take me to visit him,' Mora reminded Hamish. 'Will you, Hamish?'

'Of course, if you'd like to,' he said, though his concurrence lacked enthusiasm. He glanced at his wristwatch. 'We'll go now, if you like.' Almost as if he wanted it over and done with, she thought.

Instead of turning left at the top of the stairs as Mora did to get to her room, they turned right and walked the length of the corridor before turning right again, into another corridor. It was the first time that the true vastness of the castle had been brought home to her and she felt a sudden lilt of excitement as they walked along the wide, deep carpeted passageway, past tall windows that looked down into the courtyard, shadowed and gloomy in the dusk, and patched with yellow slashes of light from the windows.

'I had no idea it was so big,' she said, and Hamish smiled rather wryly.

'Oh yes, it's big. Far bigger than is practicable these days, I'm afraid. Staff is a problem, though we've been quite lucky and Aunt Alison's a terribly efficient organiser, though she and Nana don't always see eye to eye.'

Mora laughed, well able to imagine many differences that must arise between the rather endearingly vague Jeannie McKenzie and the hearty no-nonsense Miss McLean. She looked around her at the walls, hung with more paintings and more evidence of the past warlike McLeans. 'Is this the north wing where Bloody Adam walks?' she asked, only half seriously.

Hamish nodded to the corridor ahead of them. 'Down there in the tower room,' he said. 'He died there and he's supposed to haunt the room. Not that it's ever used now, of course. There's only Grandfather McLean and Ramsey in the north wing. Ramsey is the old man's jack of all trades,' he added by way of explanation. 'He's been here most of his life.'

They had halted outside the door of a room nearly half way along the corridor and Hamish raised a tentative hand

34

to knock. It was a second or two before the door opened a few inches and a dark-visaged head appeared, the eyes looking at Hamish with unflattering appraisal before the door opened wider to admit them.

' 'Tis Mr. Hamish an' a young lady,' he announced with complete lack of enthusiasm, as if he desired nothing so much as to be ordered to show them out again. As Mora passed him, however, he blinked in momentary surprise and looked as if he had seen a ghost, following her progress across the room before he closed the door.

There were two men in the room and Mora frowned her uneasiness when she saw the younger one. Adam McLean rose from his chair as they came in, his mouth crooked into an amused smile. He was much more formally dressed than he had been earlier in the day and the dark suit and white shirt he wore made him look even more like the other Adam McLean.

'Hamish and his Paddy,' he said, and the older man looked at Mora as if he too found her appearance hard to believe, a reaction that did nothing to put her at ease. However, a second later he smiled and held out a hand in welcome to her and Adam McLean came round the old man's chair, taking the initiative from his brother, taking Mora's hand and leading her across to the big winged armchair. 'Grandfather, this is Mora O'Connell. Paddy, my grandfather, Ian McLean.'

The man in the chair might just have warranted the title 'old', but he could have been no more than sixty-five or six, Mora guessed, but lines of pain about the eyes and mouth made him look much older at first glance. The eyes were the same startlingly bright blue as his son's and just as alert when he studied Mora with an intensity she found disturbing.

'Miss O'Connell! Welcome to Glen Ghyll.' A thin but strong hand engulfed her own and the gaunt face smiled at her. 'Don't be angry with Adam, he tries to live up to his namesake and he doesn't altogether succeed.' Adam

35

McLean, beside her, laughed softly, apparently as little put out by his grandfather's opinion of him as by anyone else's.

'I'm pleased to meet you, Mr. McLean,' smiled Mora, wondering at his family's description of him as short-tempered. He looked shrewd and alert and would probably not suffer fools gladly, but he seemed pleasant enough. Of his rather scathing remark about his grandson, she took no notice. It was good to know that someone could put Adam McLean firmly in his place.

'Hello, Grandfather.' Hamish spoke from behind her and the old man's eyes flicked on to him, narrowed slightly and with a hint of malice in them.

'Hamish! I heard you were back. Came yesterday, didn't you?' The implication was obvious and Hamish had the grace to look a little ashamed.

'Yes, Grandfather, I did. I should have come and visited you earlier, I'm sorry.'

'Oh, don't worry,' the old man assured him dryly. 'I never bother who comes and who goes as long as they don't bother me.' He turned his gaze back to Mora and smiled wickedly. 'Except when it's a pretty girl, of course, *then* I don't like to be left in the dark.' He studied her for a moment or two in silence and again Mora felt that trickle of uneasiness under the scrutiny. She could feel her colour rise and the amused eyes of Adam McLean fixed on her did nothing to help. 'You're a lovely girl, Mora O'Connell,' the old man said softly. 'A very lovely girl.'

'I told you she was,' Adam McLean said quietly, and Mora flicked a brief glance at the dark face, strangely luminous in the softly lit room, the eyes glittering with some emotion she could only guess at, but which made her shiver involuntarily.

'When are you going to marry my grandson?' the old man asked, and Mora caught her breath at the unexpectedness of it.

'I—I don't know that I am, Mr. McLean.' Mora glanced appealingly at Hamish, who looked as taken aback at his grandfather's blunt question as she was herself.

'There's nothing settled yet, Grandfather,' he said. 'Mora is writing a book, the history of the Glen Ghyll McLeans, and she's here doing research on the subject.'

'Oh?' The blue eyes looked at Mora shrewdly. 'Why us, young lady? What makes the Glen Ghyll McLeans so interesting to you?'

'Chiefly because my grandfather was a McLean,' Mora answered, and sensed rather than saw Adam's head lift interestedly. 'He came from Glen Isla.'

The two men, Adam McLean and his grandfather, exchanged glances, and Mora thought that something in her explanation had struck a note with both of them, though she could not imagine what it could be. 'Was he now?' the old man said softly. 'He'd be Robert McLean, would he not?'

'He was,' Mora agreed, realising for the first time that the girl her grandfather had eloped with all those years ago was the one the old man's father had been engaged to marry. 'I believe he was your father's cousin, Mr. McLean.'

'He was that,' the old man agreed, and unexpectedly chuckled. 'And a dastardly villain he was, so I've heard, eloping with my father's girl. Still,' he added with a wicked twinkle, 'it seems to be a family trait to covet the other men's women.'

Mora remembered the first Adam McLean and instinctively glanced across at the present holder of the name, only to find him looking at her with amused speculation as if he wondered what her reaction to the remark would be. She hastily averted her gaze. 'Not so much nowadays, I hope,' she said, and heard him laugh softly.

'Mebbe so, mebbe so,' Ian McLean said slowly, and eyed Mora again with a hint of smile round his mouth. 'You'll be a girl who knows her own mind, no doubt, Mora?' He gave the name a soft, almost caressing sound and Mora wondered how much he had once been like his favourite grandson. There was a certain air of impudence even now in his manner that could have been just like

Adam McLean's years ago.

'I think I do,' she said cautiously, and glanced briefly at Hamish, who looked down at his feet and refused to lend his support.

'I can see you do,' the old man insisted with a smile. 'You've enough of the McLean blood to know what you want and go after it.'

Adam was studying her with that amused gaze still, and she felt a prickle of resentment when she caught his eye. 'Oh, she's a McLean,' he said softly. 'You can see the look in her eyes, can't you? That touch of arrogance.'

Mora coloured angrily at his scrutiny. 'I leave the arrogance to you, Mr. McLean,' she told him coldly, and heard the old man chuckle delightedly.

'Don't mind us too much, my dear,' he said gently, taking her hands in both of his. 'We're not as bad as you may think. I hope you'll spare me some more of your time while you're here,' he added, a mite wistfully, Mora thought. 'I know as much of the family history as anybody does and I could help you quite a lot if you'd like me to.'

'Thank you,' she said warmly, instinctively liking the old man, though she had no such feeling for his grandson.

'I hope we don't prove too much of a disappointment to you,' Ian McLean went on. 'We've had a long but not too eventful history, though there were the usual scatterings of villainy, of course. Every family has them.' He cocked an enquiring eye at her. 'You've heard of Bloody Adam, of course?'

'Er—yes. This morning,' Mora admitted. 'Hamish and Mrs. Fergus McLean were telling me about him and later I found him in the portrait collection.'

'And she thought she was seeing ghosts when I spoke to her,' Adam said, smiling wickedly at the recollection.

'He's the only *really* bad lot we've produced,' the old man told her, 'and he probably had extenuating circumstances. One always gets a rather trimmed up version from history, I think. Black is black and white is white, there

38

never seems to be a nice, human greyness about any of them.' He glanced at his two grandsons and a wry smile touched the thin straight mouth. 'I wonder how we'll all come out of it in two hundred years' time.'

'I—I don't know,' said Mora, when neither of them answered him. 'Probably no better or worse than any of the other generations.'

'Ah, I expect you're right, my dear.' There was an unutterable weariness in the old man's voice and Adam McLean moved round to stand beside his grandfather, his eyes anxious as he looked at the drawn face and pain-lined forehead.

'Oh, I do hope I haven't stayed too long and tired you,' Mora said anxiously, putting a hand gently on the old man's arm and wishing that Adam McLean would not look at her with that surprised and grateful look that made her feel uneasy.

'Of course you haven't,' Ian McLean assured her with a smile, but the lines around his eyes and mouth were far more pronounced than when she first saw him, she felt sure, and in the soft light of a well-shaded lamp he looked a very sick man and a very old one.

'I think we'd better go, Grandfather,' Hamish said, and sounded relieved at the prospect of ending the visit. 'It's getting late and you need your rest.'

'Rest is something I get plenty of,' his grandfather told him a little tartly. 'It's not often I have a pretty visitor to cheer me. You will come again, won't you, Mora?'

'I'd like to,' Mora said softly and with sincerity. 'I'm glad I've met you, Mr. McLean, and I look forward to your help with the family history.'

The old man chuckled despite his tiredness, and his head shook slowly as if the prospect pleased him enormously. 'We'll rake up every scandal that ever sullied the family's name,' he promised with barely suppressed glee. 'We'll have a rare time, Mora, you'll see.'

The uncommunicative Ramsey, the manservant, let them

out of the room and Mora thought she caught a glimpse of laughter in the narrow eyes when they looked at her, but the gaze was lowered so hastily that she could not be sure. There was, however, no doubt about Adam McLean's expression when she turned in the doorway to smile at the old man. He looked maliciously amused and she wondered if she could ever grow to like him as she did the rest of his family.

Although Hamish had spoken of the lateness of the hour, it was not in fact, very late and he and Fergus, with their father, decided to have a rubber or two of bridge before bedtime. Mora was invited to make a fourth but, being a very inexperienced player, she declined, and Alison McLean joined her brother and her two nephews at the table.

'You don't mind?' Hamish asked before the game began, and Mora shook her head.

'Of course I don't mind,' she told him. 'I shall stroll down the drive a little way before I go up and wish on the new moon.'

'Wish for me,' Hamish whispered to her as she paused by his chair, and she smiled.

'I will,' she promised.

'Don't get lost,' Sir James warned her, half in jest. 'We'd probably never find you at this time of night.'

'I won't,' Mora promised with a smile. 'If I stay near the trees down the drive, I shall be all right.'

She left the room and crossed to the stairs to fetch a coat and something for her head against the cold wind, mounting the wide staircase with that ever-present feeling of grandeur it gave her.

Reaching the top, she paused when she heard footsteps along the corridor to her right, uneasy for a moment about the ghost of Adam McLean. It was Adam McLean, but the living holder of the name, and she would have turned along the corridor to her room without speaking if he had not called out to her.

40

'Mora!' Faced with a direct address, she could do little else but wait for him to join her at the top of the stairs. 'You're an early bird,' he told her, 'and it isn't because you need your beauty sleep!'

She ignored the compliment and pondered on the wisdom of telling him her intention. 'I'm going for a walk,' she said, stiffly formal. 'I came up for a coat.'

He looked at her steadily for a moment, without the customary amusement glittering in his eyes. 'It's not the time of the year for night walks,' he said. 'But if it's a breath of air you want, why not walk out on the south tower for a few minutes? That'll blow away any cobwebs.'

'The *south* tower?' She was uncertain of the seriousness of his suggestion or the motive behind it, but curiosity overcame her suspicion of him for the moment. 'Not where —where the other Adam McLean walks?'

His laugh had a deep soft sound to it and she felt a tingle of warning trickle along her spine at the sound of it. 'Do you believe that Bloody Adam walks the north tower?' he asked, and she flushed at the teasing look in his eyes, angry that she had laid such a trap for herself.

'No—no, of course not,' she denied, 'but it's a good story.'

'Would you like to put it to the test?' It was a challenge, she knew, and she almost responded in the way her nature prompted her to, but she had no desire to be in the company of both Adam McLeans, should the first one also choose to put in an appearance.

'No,' she said, 'I'm not dressed for ghost hunting.'

'The south tower, then?' he suggested, and she hesitated only briefly before nodding agreement. 'You'll still need a coat, the wind is terrific out there. I'll wait for you at the end of the corridor while you fetch it.'

As she put on a thick warm coat, she wondered about her hasty acquiescence to his suggestion and decided that it was as much her curiosity as for any other reason that she was visiting the south tower. The two solid-looking towers

41

squaring the front of the castle were what, in Mora's opinion, made it seem like a real castle. There was something irresistible about turreted castles that stemmed from fairy stories as a child, she supposed, and she felt a tingle of excitement at the prospect of actually visiting one, though what Hamish would say if he knew in whose company she was going, she tried not to think.

The atmosphere could not have been more conducive to shudders had they really been ghost-hunting, for none of the rooms along the south side of the castle were occupied and the long corridor was unlit. There was lighting available, but her guide made no effort to switch it on and they had only the fitful and wan light of the new moon as they walked down the wide passageway, their tread muffled by the carpet underfoot.

Past the closed doors of the unused rooms and right to the end of the corridor where a stout oak door barred the way of further progress. Without a word, Adam McLean turned the big wrought-iron ring that served as a handle and opened the door.

Mora hesitated as the damp, stale smell of age and disuse tingled in her nostrils and her heart thudded uncomfortably hard against her ribs. 'Come on,' her guide encouraged, and she could imagine the mocking challenge in his eyes although it was too dark for her to see it. 'Scared?' he added softly as she still hesitated.

'No, of course not!' she retorted, and stepped into the room, albeit cautiously. It was L-shaped, with the door in the short leg of the L, and tall slit windows let in the pale moonlight in thin slivers that shimmered across the stone floor.

'Cosy, isn't it?' he asked, and she could not have agreed less. There was a cold dank atmosphere in the place that seemed pregnant with anticipation of heaven knew what, and she shivered again involuntarily. He stood just behind her in the doorway as she looked around the bare, chill room. 'It's said that Adam and his lady-love used to meet here,' he told her, his breath stirring the tendrils of hair in her neck as he spoke close to her ear. 'Though how they managed to get so far without being spotted, I don't know.'

'It must have been dangerous,' she ventured, determined not to betray her nervousness, both of the room and of him. 'I wonder *some*one didn't see them.'

'I suppose someone did,' he said, 'or we should never have known about it today. But Adam was a daring man and believed in taking chances.' He chuckled in the darkness beside her. 'The cuckolded Robert and his wife lived here with him, I suppose that made things easier for them. They must have appeared quite a devoted couple, Robert and Marjorie, to anyone who didn't know their story. They had a family of seven.'

'Seven!' Mora echoed, and added, 'Of course they had large families in those days, didn't they?'

'So I believe,' he agreed dryly. 'They had six girls and one boy. And his paternity was in some doubt, I should say, judging by the looks *I've* inherited.'

'I see,' was all the comment she made, and he chuckled again as if her reserve amused him.

'To your left,' he told her, 'you'll find some steps, but you'd better let me go first as you're not used to them.' He walked past her, like a shadow in the moonlight, and vanished from her sight, only to reappear a second later, his teeth gleaming whitely against the darkness of his face as he smiled at her. 'This way,' he said. 'Give me your hand—and watch your step, some of the stairs are a bit worn in places.'

The stone staircase was very narrow and dark, twisting half-way up to turn back on itself. At the top they stepped out into the coldness of the night air and a wind that lifted Mora's hair and set it flying about her face. The wall surrounding the tower was waist high and solid enough to be reassuring when she looked down over the edge at the ground far below. It was comfortingly light up here after the darkness of the stairs and she could easily distinguish the driveway with its guard of tall, bare trees and the distant glint of the loch and its attendant pools.

'It's a wonderful view from up here,' she said. 'It must be even better on a sunny day.'

'Oh, I don't know,' he demurred. 'I like the moonlit view best. It has a certain atmosphere of mystery about it.' She could see his face better now that there was more light, but it was difficult to judge the expression in his eyes and she was uncertain how serious he was. He stood close beside her and she could feel the tense energy of him as he leaned over the edge of the surrounding wall and looked down.

'Be careful!' she begged automatically, and he turned his head and looked at her in surprise.

'I won't fall,' he said, and again she was uncertain how serious he was. 'But I'm flattered that you're concerned for my safety.'

The inevitable prick of resentment sharpened her voice when she replied. 'I'm not particularly,' she retorted, 'but it seems a pity to spoil such a lovely night with an accident.'

He was silent for a moment and then she heard the deep sound of his laughter again. 'Are you really Hamish's girl?' he asked. 'I find it very hard to believe, you've too much spirit for brother Hamish, surely.'

'I am *not* Hamish's girl,' she told him crossly. 'At least not in the way you mean. I told your grandfather tonight. I don't know whether I *am* going to marry Hamish or not yet.'

'He's asked you to?' He was definitely serious now, she thought.

'Yes, he has.'

'Hmm.' The deep grey eyes looked fathomless in the wan light, fathomless and a little ominous as the water in the loch had done that morning. 'You've made quite a hit with the old man, you know. He doesn't always take kindly to strangers, but he liked you. Of course,' he added almost as if to himself, 'you're special.'

She looked puzzled. 'How special?' she asked, and he

44

smiled, shaking his head at her.

'Never mind,' he said. 'But you will go and see him again as you promised, won't you?'

'Of course I will,' she replied, surprised at his earnestness. 'If it won't tire him too much. He looked very ill and rather frail.'

'He's in pain,' he said abruptly, 'and he's not always as sociable as he might be, that's why the family usually leave him to his own devices. They pay him a duty visit occasionally as Hamish did tonight.' He looked at her steadily for a moment. 'Or was tonight's visit your idea?'

'In a way,' she admitted, unwilling to lose Hamish even this little favour in his brother's eyes. 'It—it was a sort of mutual idea.' She saw his look of disbelief and hastened on, 'Anyway, I'm glad I came.'

'I'm glad you did too, and not only for Grandfather's sake.'

She wished she could determined how serious he was and tried again to read the expression in his eyes, but found it impossible. 'I like your grandfather,' she said. 'And I'd like to see him again if it really won't be too much for him.'

'It won't,' he assured her. 'It will give him something to look forward to. As I told you before, he likes lovely women and you're very lovely.'

Again his unexpected flattery deprived her of an immediate answer. There was none of Hamish's earnest and gentle courtesy about the compliments he paid her. Each time she felt he was offering her a challenge and she could do little to stop the strange excitement that stirred in her. He was perhaps too dangerously like his ancestral namesake and, remembering *his* reputation, she told herself she was a fool to have come to this lonely, disused wing of the castle with him.

'I—I think I'd like to go now, if you don't mind,' she said, and as if he suspected her reasons, he chuckled softly in the semi-dark.

'Already?' He sounded disappointed, but she could make

out the crook of a smile at the corners of his mouth. He leaned nearer to her, his voice deep and filled with laughter. 'You wouldn't be afraid of me, would you, Paddy O'Connell?'

'Don't call me Paddy!' she said crossly. 'I don't like it.'

'Well, it certainly suits you,' he retorted. 'I never saw such an Irish firecracker.'

She would have liked nothing better than to have hit him hard across his dark arrogant face, but that, she thought, was probably exactly what he expected her to do, and she would not give him the satisfaction of being right. Instead she kept a firm control on her temper, only a slight tremble in her voice betraying her effort. 'Perhaps your experience is limited, Mr. McLean. And I'm *not* Irish. I'm English by birth and upbringing.'

'But blood will out,' he retorted with a laugh. 'And you've not only got an Irish paddy, you've got the McLean one too.' He eyed her angry face for a moment curiously. 'How *did* you meet Hamish?' he asked.

She drew a deep breath before she replied, trying to keep control of her anger. 'I met him at an art gallery. A new one, it was the opening, actually.'

'Are you an arty type?' he asked, looking vaguely surprised.

'No. But I like paintings. Some paintings,' she added hastily.

'And Hamish took advantage of his good luck?' He laughed softly. 'Good old Hamish, I never thought he had it in him.'

'Do you have to be so patronising about Hamish?' she asked shortly. 'He's charming and very good-mannered.'

'Oh, I'm sure he is,' he agreed solemnly. 'And he thinks I'm no better than I should be, which is an opinion that is most heartily endorsed by you, I suspect.'

'I—I haven't had time to form an opinion,' she said cautiously, his sudden switch to a more personal theme making her uneasy again. 'I didn't even know you existed until this morning and you haven't been at meals so I haven't had an opportunity to judge.'

'Oh, I don't live at the castle,' he said blithely, and grinned at her expression of surprise. 'There's a little cottage at the back which you can just see from your window. I live there.'

'But——' Her curiosity almost compelled her to ask outright about the reason that kept him isolated from his family and he seemed to sense it.

'Now you're more mystified than ever,' he chuckled. 'Well, it's quite simple really. I'm the black sheep of the family, as I told you this morning, and as such I'm not mentioned in polite society, but as—as a son I do have certain rights, and a home at Glen Ghyll is one of them.'

'It's—it's a very close family,' she said, trying to read the expression in his eyes in the deceptive light. 'And it must be an enormous responsibility being the head of it.'

'I imagine so,' he agreed solemnly enough. 'At the moment Grandfather is the head man, although Father does most of the active part of it these days.'

Mora looked out again at the moonlit scene below them. 'Poor Hamish,' she said softly. 'It must be quite a prospect knowing that one day he'll be responsible for all this and so much more besides.'

'The heir to the estate,' he said, and she could hear the mockery in his voice. 'Is *that* his attraction?' Her anger held her tongue, but her eyes blazed at him furiously and he stepped back in mock alarm, his hands raised defensively. 'Whoa!' he laughed. 'You look ready to explode, Paddy.'

'You are ins*uff*erable!' she burst out angrily at last. 'And I refuse to stay here any longer and listen to your—your arrogance!' She turned away from the wind and the moonlight and towards the narrow doorway from which they had emerged and which looked dismayingly black and frightening. She stood hesitant in the doorway, and heard him laugh softly behind her.

47

'Mind your neck,' he teased her. 'You could quit easily break it if you fall down those stairs.'

She turned and looked at him over her shoulder, dark and insolent and daring her to step through that forbidding opening. For a second or two they stood like shadows, only the wind stirring hair and clothing to give them movement, then he strode round behind her and disappeared into the blackness of the tower.

'Give me your hand,' he ordered as she stepped through after him, but she shook her head obstinately, her fingers groping on the cold stone walls on either side of her, feeling her way down the worn, narrow stairs. She had almost reached the bottom without mishap, when she trod on a step more worn than the rest and felt herself falling, her hands groping in vain for the reassuring solidity of the walls.

She was only three or four steps from the bottom and her companion was already standing in the moonlit room, turning to watch her descent, so that it took him only a split second to be in place to break her fall, his arms tight around her as she fell against him. For a moment she was too breathless to move or make a sound and before she could recover she saw the dark shadow of his head bend over her and his mouth sought hers unerringly.

The kiss was brief and light-hearted and he chuckled at her murmur of protest. 'Shades of the original Adam,' he said. 'I couldn't resist it.'

CHAPTER FOUR

As far as possible Mora avoided Adam McLean, but it was difficult when she spent so much time with old Ian McLean. At least half a dozen times in the next two weeks she had either found him already with his grandfather when she visited him or he had joined them very shortly afterwards. The old man seemed to relish their inevitable arguments and he chuckled gleefully whenever Mora managed to score off his grandson which, she had to admit, was all too infrequently.

She liked Ian McLean's company and even appreciated his rather malicious pleasure in her own and Adam's attitude to one another, for he had a lively mind and must have found the years of enforced confinement very irksome. She had accumulated a vast store of knowledge since talking to the old man and found her ancestral history even more interesting than she had anticipated.

She rode quite often, even though the weather was discouraging with the year growing old, but it was so far without snow and not yet wet enough to be dangerous. Hamish usually managed to come with her, but when he was busy she either went alone or, as happened once or twice, Fergus accompanied her. It was, she thought, almost as if they feared her meeting with their brother alone.

Once, when she was out alone, she had met Helen Murdoe and the other girl had greeted her with a rather chilling reserve, the wide dark eyes coldly appraising Mora's slim figure and wind-flushed face. It was not an encounter she wanted to repeat.

This morning Hamish was required at a business meeting

in Cairndale and Mora decided to ride alone since she herself had no objection at all to her own company. She collected the grey she invariably rode from the lugubrious Rob Smith and tried, as usual, to bring a smile to the dour face, failing inevitably as she always did.

There was a pale, wintry-looking sun after a slight frost and everywhere looked and smelled clean and sparkling. She decided she would ride down as far as the village and return via the far side of the loch, following the stream back to Glen Ghyll. It was a fairly long ride, but the morning was clear and dry and it would do neither her nor Mist, the grey, any harm to breathe some of the good fresh air that Miss Alison McLean was so enthusiastic about.

The village of Glencairn was about a mile away and built at the very end of the long glen, with a hill rising up behind it like a protective wall. From the same hill the stream started its journey as a sparkling fall, fed by the rain and snow, rushing down the hillside until it became more leisurely further down the glen. It was a picture-postcard village and Mora never tired of looking at it.

She approached the collection of stone houses slowly, for Mist was not an animal who liked to be hurried even with the sting of frost to encourage him. The first house, standing alone and slightly apart from the others, was Cairn House, the home of Helen Murdoe and her mother, and she fervently hoped that she would not meet the other girl again. With the prospect uppermost in her mind, she turned the grey before she reached the large, rather gloomy-looking house and set off along the side of the loch, letting the animal set his own pace.

She had gone perhaps fifty yards when she saw the woman she had hoped to avoid and frowned her annoyance. Helen Murdoe was coming in the opposite direction and it was useless to hope that she had not seen her. Tall and graceful in the saddle, she rode a beautiful bay that needed a firm hand, and Mora could not help but admire the way she handled the strong animal.

The girl's dark eyes looked at Mora with the same chilling lack of welcome as before and Mora would simply have exchanged brief greetings and passed by, but Helen Murdoe reined in the bay so that it blocked the path and Mora was obliged to do the same. There was a trace of a smile round the wide mouth as she sat facing Mora, a chilling smile that was in no way friendly.

'You'll be taking the long way back, Miss O'Connell?' she asked in her soft voice, and Mora nodded. 'You'd much better turn back the way you came or you'll be caught in a downpour.'

Mora glanced up at the pale sky and pallid sun and smiled her disbelief, though there were some grey clouds in the distance, rolling nearer every minute on the brisk wind. She would surely have ample time to get back to Glen Ghyll before the rain broke. 'I think I'll chance it,' she said, smiling at the unfriendly face, and saw the flush of colour that touched the high cheekbones. 'Thank you for the warning, Miss Murdoe.'

'You'll not change your mind and turn about?'

'I don't think so. I think I might be able to get back before it starts.' She had a strange intuition that there was some other reason than the threat of rain why Helen Murdoe wanted her to turn back, and that in itself was enough to send Mora on the path she had chosen.

'You're a stubborn one,' the soft voice informed her with an edge of harshness in its usually gentle timbre. 'Adam said you were.'

Mora flushed at the idea of being discussed by Adam McLean and this unfriendly girl and she bit her lip not to be unforgivably rude about it. 'I know quite well that Adam McLean has a very low opinion of me,' she said stiffly, 'but I care neither one way nor the other. However, I do object to being the subject of your discussions and I'd be obliged if you'd leave me out of them in future.'

'Adam is a shrewd judge of character,' Helen Murdoe said, a smile round her mouth that was sharp with malice.

51

'He finds you a great source of amusement and I'm afraid he doesn't always keep it to himself.'

Mora could visualise the two of them laughing over some quarrel she had had with Adam McLean and Adam with his mocking eyes watching her and remembering everything she did so that he could relate it to Helen Murdoe. She found it almost impossible not to deliberately quarrel with the girl, but instead she swallowed hard on her anger and was coolly polite.

'If you'll excuse me, Miss Murdoe, I'd like to go on.' She turned the reluctant Mist and skirted round the other girl, who stood for a moment uncertain and frustrated. After a moment or two she put her heels to the mettlesome bay and galloped off towards the lonely-looking house where she lived, and Mora turned and watched her go, still puzzled as to why she had wanted her to turn and go back the way she had come, still more puzzled by her obvious desire to quarrel with her.

She found all thought of Hamish and his proposal of last night put clean out of her mind by the idea of Adam McLean and Helen Murdoe discussing her as they did. She had to admit that she was enjoying her stay at Glen Ghyll enormously, but how much longer she would be able to stay and still keep Hamish at a distance she had no idea. It was becoming more and more difficult to remain unmoved by his obvious determination to marry her and now that she knew how Adam was behaving about her, she would never again feel as comfortable, even with the old man for company. For the moment she felt she hated Adam McLean for spoiling everything, and she sighed so that the grey tossed his head in sympathy as he picked his way over the stones at the edge of the loch.

A gradual darkening of the sky warned her that Helen Murdoe's estimated time for the storm had been a better forecast than her own and she made a rueful face as she put her heels to the plodding animal and brought him up to a trot.

She had gone very little further before the storm broke and even the easy-going Mist increased his pace without encouragement. It was as if the heavens had opened up and the rain simply poured down, so that she could see only a few yards ahead and the horse's ears were flat and low to shut out the stinging hiss and fury of it. There was no sheltering rock or hill in this part of the flat glen and she shook her head, angry that Helen Murdoe had been so right and that her own stubbornness had prevented her from being at least a little nearer home.

It was difficult to hear anything above the wind and the rain, but she was sure suddenly that she heard the flinty click of another horse coming over the stony ground at a much faster pace than her own was travelling, and she half turned her head to look over her right shoulder.

Through the haze of rain she could make out a crouched figure, on a horse that came galloping towards her, ears flat, tail and mane streaming out, the flying hooves sending up spray and tiny clods of turf from the ground. It took her only a second to recognise both horse and rider, and by then Adam McLean's voice shouted at her above the storm. 'Follow me!'

Almost automatically she obeyed, urging Mist on to greater effort, though she doubted if he could match the tremendous pace of the other, a wickedly strong black. They veered right, away from the loch, and after a few moments her guide raised one hand briefly before he reined his animal to a halt before a tiny stone hut with the remains of a lean-to outhouse at one side of it.

He took the reins from her and led the two animals into the shelter of the outhouse, while Mora approached the door of the hut uncertainly. It looked empty, but she raised a hand and knocked on the stout wooden door. When there was no reply, she lifted the latch tentatively and stepped inside. It was deserted, that was obvious, but it was dry and even struck slightly warmer as she looked around her.

There was one window, at the same side as the door, and an old stone fireplace with an iron arm for suspending a cooking pot. There was even wood beside the hearth and the blackened stone hearth looked recently used.

A moment later Adam McLean joined her, slamming the door behind him and pulling off his dripping wet jacket as he crossed the room towards the fireplace. 'Find some paper,' he said brusquely, 'there'll be some in that box in the corner, and get that wet coat off.'

'I'll be warmer with it on,' she argued automatically, and he glanced up at her with a look of resignation in his eyes.

'All right,' he said, 'get pneumonia if you want to, but don't blame me.' He turned back to his task of breaking the dry wood into usable lengths and apparently did not notice her take off her wet coat and hang it on a nail driven into the wooden door-post.

She found paper, as he said she would, and brought it to him, crumpling it into rough balls so that it would burn more easily and ignite the wood. The blaze was bright and cheerful and he saw it burning to his satisfaction before going to a cupboard in one corner of the room and pulling out an armful of logs.

Mora watched the proceedings with some surprise and at last he looked up at her with a smile. 'Everything seems to be to hand,' she said. 'I hadn't even noticed this little place before, and I've been round this way more than once.'

His hands placed the logs carefully on top of the blaze. 'I expect you were otherwise occupied,' he said wryly, and the light of mockery was in his eyes again so that she stiffened in her customary defence, remembering again that he would probably tell everything to Helen Murdoe when he next saw her.

'I was with Hamish,' she said, 'but I was still capable of noticing my surroundings; it must blend into its surroundings pretty well. Who does it belong to?'

'Anyone who gets caught like we have,' he told her,

54

fetching their two jackets and putting them near the fire to dry. 'Strictly speaking it's part of the Glen Ghyll property. It's always kept supplied with wood and some tinned food and it can be very useful in the worst of winter.'

'I can imagine,' she said. 'I don't think either Mist or I could have gone for much longer in this.'

'You were taking a chance coming so far,' he informed her with his customary lack of tact, and she flushed angrily at the criticism, her deep blue eyes glinting in the light of the fire.

The fact that she had been warned did not make his remark any more welcome. '*You* were caught,' she reminded him, 'and you should surely have known better. unless,' she added, remembering the direction Helen Murdoe had been coming from, 'you had a rendezvous that you had to keep.'

He eyed her speculatively for a moment, his hands thrust into the pockets of his riding breeches, standing in that characteristic attitude he invariably adopted—feet apart, head slightly back, relaxed and confident. 'I have a feeling you're being ambiguous,' he said, a glint of mockery in his eyes that made her feel more than ever uneasy.

'I'm not,' she denied, and he laughed, turning to pull up to the fire, a rough bench that stood against the wall. He brushed it off carefully with a handkerchief and bobbed her a half bow, extending one hand in invitation.

'Sit down,' he said, 'and I'll make some coffee. It'll be powdered, but it'll be hot and maybe take the chill out of the situation.' He ignored her glare of reproach and laughed. 'Besides,' he added, 'you look like a drowned rabbit.'

'Thank you.' She resented his tactless reference to her wet hair and bedraggled appearance and hastily pulled off the scarf that had done little to protect her head. Sitting on the bench before the fire she bent her head towards the heat and ruffled her hair with her fingers. Its usual soft curls when wet became tight and clung to her head closely, looking darker than usual.

'On second thoughts,' he informed her from the far corner of the room, 'I've never seen a curly rabbit, perhaps a labrador would be more apt.'

'You *are* insufferable,' she said chillingly, glaring over her shoulder at him and hastily lowering her gaze when she met the laughter in his eyes. His own thick hair, she noticed, was even wetter than hers and he impatiently brushed away drops of moisture as he took an iron kettle from a cupboard above the one that held the logs, and filled it from a covered barrel in the opposite corner.

He brought the kettle across to the fire and deftly hooked it on to the swinging arm over the blaze, bending over to reach the hook and peering up into her face as she sat with bent head, her face flushed from the heat. 'Sugar?' he enquired politely, 'or are you sweet enough?'

'Sugar, please,' she said. 'Two.'

'Black or white?'

She hesitated, looking at him suspiciously to know whether he was teasing her or not. 'There can't be any milk,' she said at last. 'Can there?'

He nodded. 'Dried, but I can put plenty in if that's how you like it.'

'Thank you,' she said, unusually demure. 'I like it very white if I may.' He bobbed his head and drew back out of her sight, while she still kept her head bent, wondering at the sudden and rapid thudding of her heart against her ribs.

The coffee was not the best she had ever tasted, but it was blissfully warm as she held the thick mug between her hands and swallowed mouthfuls of warmth. 'All right?' he asked, and she nodded.

'Lovely, thank you.' She glanced from under her long lashes at the dark face, looking uncharacteristically relaxed in the flickering light of the fire.

There were fine lines at the corners of his eyes and his slightly crooked mouth and the firelight played tricks with her vision so that at times he looked remarkably like Ian

McLean and at others like the robust alertness of his father. It was a changing and expressive face and, she had to admit, an interesting one.

He turned his head and looked at her, almost as if he suspected her preoccupation with him. 'Are you cold?' he asked, and she shook her head.

'Not now, the coffee was just what I needed.' She looked around the tiny room, almost cosy in the flickering light of the fire. Anything to avoid meeting his eyes. 'This could be made into quite a snug little home,' she opined. 'It's tiny, of course, but it's surprisingly warm with the fire burning and it's dry.'

'You could set up home here if you like,' he offered, and she chanced a brief look of reproach at him. 'I'm sorry, but you did seem quite taken with it.'

'You can never resist trying to make me look small, can you?' she asked, and was surprised that she felt rather like crying.

'Not at all,' he denied. 'I can't resist teasing you if that's what you mean, it's not the same at all.' She did not answer him but stared into the crackling blaze of the fire. 'Why are you always so nervous with me?' The question was so unexpected that she stared at him for a moment, wide-eyed and unanswering.

'I—I don't know that I am,' she said cautiously, wishing she could control the dizzying throb of pulse in her head and the way her fingers trembled as they held the thick mug.

'Oh, but you are,' he insisted, and put a hand to gently touch the throbbing pulse in her temple. 'Why, Mora?'

'I'm *not*,' she argued, gripping the mug more firmly. 'Please don't——'

'All right, all right!' He laughed softly and withdrew the touch she found so disturbing. 'I won't question you if you don't know the answer.' She knew he still watched her, though she kept her eyes averted, staring into the fire. 'Poor Hamish,' he said after a second or two, and it was almost as if he spoke to himself.

She did not question his meaning but drank her coffee slowly, her mind racing with a thousand and one things, none of them to do with Hamish.

She wondered if Adam *had* been out to meet Helen Murdoe and if he had, just how close their relationship was. The girl evidently did not share his family's disapproval of him, for she had made only favourable comment on his powers of judgment and implied that he shared his amusement with her. The latter thought made her frown as she remembered how they must have been discussing her and she hated the thought more than she admitted.

'I met Miss Murdoe just before the rain started,' she said, and glanced at him surreptitiously from under her lashes, hastily shifting her gaze when he looked at her.

'Helen?' he said. 'Did you?' He sounded uninterested, but that could have been deliberate.

'She—she told me you were a very good judge of character,' she ventured, and saw his dark brows rise at the information.

'Oh? Now what possessed her to make a remark like that out of the blue?' he said, looking at her speculatively over the top of his coffee mug.

'It—it wasn't really out of the blue exactly,' she confessed. 'She warned me to take the short way home and I——'

'And you declined,' he interposed with a wry grin. 'Yes, you would, of course.'

'I thought I had time to come this way,' she said defensively, running her fingers through the half dry curls until they tumbled about her face and gave her a gamin look enhanced by a smut from the fire, on one cheek. 'She said you told her I was stubborn,' she added accusingly.

'Did I?'

'Well, *did* you?' She looked at him defiantly, only inches away thanks to the shortness of the bench, and he laughed.

'Perhaps,' he admitted, 'I don't remember.'

'Well, I wish you'd refrain from discussing me with all and sundry,' she protested crossly. 'She said you found me amusing too—well, I know you do, but you don't have to repeat everything to—to—your——' She hesitated to use the term girl-friend because there was a look in his eyes that warned her she was treading on delicate ground and she had no desire to find out how he would be in a temper.

'My what?' he asked softly, his eyes on her flushed face and lowered lashes. 'Go on, Mora, tell me what I get up to, I'd love to know.'

'Oh, nothing!' she said crossly. She drank the last of her coffee and put the mug down on the hearth, getting to her feet and walking to the one small window the room possessed, suddenly and inexplicably afraid of her own feelings. 'It's almost stopped raining,' she said irrelevantly, and he laughed.

'You never cease to surprise me, Paddy.' He joined her beside the window so that she dared not turn round for being so near to him. 'Now you have me meeting Helen in secret rendezvous.'

'Well, weren't you with her?' she challenged, taking a chance and turning round, only to find him even closer than she feared, and he was laughing as he looked down at her bright angry face.

'Suppose I was,' he asked. 'Would it matter?'

'Not to me!' she retorted.

'Then to who? Or should it be whom?' The deep grey eyes glinted down at her wickedly, well aware of the uneasiness he caused her, and when she did not reply, he shook his head and put out a hand to wind one stray curl of her hair round a finger. 'Tell me, Paddy,' he said softly.

'No one as as far as I know,' she confessed, terribly conscious of her racing heart again and afraid he might sense it being so close, but he merely smiled and moved away, back towards the fire, where he put a booted foot on a almost spent log and flattened it into a shower of sparks.

'We'd better go,' he said as he picked up their still damp jackets from the hearth, 'before Hamish gets back from Cairndale and starts wondering about you.'

'Why should he?' she asked, on the defensive again, and he smiled at her, shaking his head slowly.

'You know perfectly well why, Paddy, don't be obtuse.' He looked back at the remains of their fire. 'I'll send Rob out here tomorrow to restock and check everything's all right.'

'In case you want to use it again?' she asked as he helped her into her jacket.

'Or anyone else,' he agreed, lifting the soft curls from her neck and twining them round his fingers.

'It's a good place for a rendezvous,' she ventured, again thinking of Helen Murdoe, and he tugged gently at the curls he held, laughing at her barely concealed curiosity.

'You never give up, do you?' he said. 'Come on, Paddy O'Connell, let's restore you to brother Hamish's loving arms before another storm starts.'

She contented herself with a black glare at him as they left the little hut, refusing to argue further about Hamish and her own relationship with him. If his affair with Helen Murdoe was no concern of hers, then the same went for her and Hamish as far as *he* was concerned.

The rain had stopped when they rode away from the hut, but the sky was dark-browed and menacing and would not remain dry for long. They returned to the castle from the back and Rob Smith met them in the stable yard, frowning disapproval over the wet animals as he led them away. 'The horses are far more important than we are, as far as Rob's concerned,' Adam commented as the stable boy moved out of earshot. 'He takes care of them like children, especially Klonda, although he's a villain.'

'Klonda? The one you were riding?' Mora asked. 'He looks pretty strong.'

'He is,' he said grimly. 'He's the one that threw my grandfather three years ago. He was even harder to handle

60

then than he is now.'

'But you still ride him?' She looked at the stubborn chin and the almost ruthless face and knew that it would be a challenge he could not resist.

He looked at her and grinned knowingly. 'The devil looks after his own,' he told her. 'I shall die in my bed like a gentleman, as the first Adam did.' He laughed softly as he turned away and for some reason Mora felt a trickle of fear run coldly along her spine. 'Au revoir, Mora.' He waved a casual hand as he went and she turned to pass through the narrow archway into the courtyard.

Hamish was absent from lunch and she thought wryly that Adam need not have bothered about his brother's worrying about her. He was there for dinner, however, and so was Helen Murdoe, much to Hamish's obvious discomfort. His conversation at dinner was spasmodic and rather absent-minded as if he found the girl's being there disturbing.

It was the first time Mora had seen the other girl at Glen Ghyll since the day of her arrival and she wondered who had been responsible for inviting her. Clearly it was not Hamish, and she could not imagine even the hearty Sir James being insensitive enough to invite her when he could see that his son found her presence so upsetting. Mora was curious, too, to know just why Hamish should find Helen Murdoe so distracting. If she was, as Mora suspected Adam McLean's paramour she should not, surely, affect Hamish in the way she did.

Mora had spent the afternoon with Ian McLean in his room, so it was not until she came down to dinner that she realised the other girl was there. 'It was kind of you to ask me to stay to dinner,' Helen Murdoe told Miss McLean in her soft, deceptively gentle voice. 'I should have gone sooner, but we did rather get involved in our conversation, didn't we, Miss McLean?'

'Indeed we did,' Alison McLean agreed, though a little reservedly, Mora thought. 'I could scarcely let you leave the house so close on dinner-time, my dear Helen. What *would* happen to the McLean reputation for hospitality?'

So that was it! The girl had outstayed an afternoon visit and the older woman had been obliged to invite her to dinner, but what Helen Murdoe's object had been in getting herself invited she could not guess. It was not as if Adam took his meals with the family.

'You'll still be busy on your book?' The soft voice addressed itself to Mora and she hastily recalled her wandering thoughts.

'Yes, that's right,' she agreed. 'Mr. McLean's been most helpful. Mr. Ian McLean, I mean,' she added hastily lest she should give the wrong impression.

'And will you be carrying on with the writing after you're married?' Mora stared at her for a moment in silence, appalled at the idea of having to answer so personal a question in front of the whole family. Hamish, she was aware, was watching her closely as if he too was anxious to hear her answer.

'I really don't know,' Mora said quietly, despite the slight tremble in her voice. 'I'm not thinking of marrying at the moment, Miss Murdoe, so the question doesn't arise yet.'

The fine dark eyes rounded with a surprise that Mora felt sure was assumed as the girl looked from Hamish to herself and back again. 'I'm sorry,' she apologised softly. 'I must have misunderstood. I thought that Hamish and you—I'm so sorry.'

There was a moment's silence which Sir James broke with one of his hearty laughs, covering his own embarrassment as well as his son's. 'It'll be no fault of Hamish's if she doesn't change her mind, eh, my dear?'

Mora smiled, her face flushed rosily. 'Perhaps, Sir James. I really don't know my own mind at the moment, so I can scarcely know what Hamish's plans are.'

'You know them well enough,' Hamish told her, unexpectedly harsh-voiced as he looked at her across the table.

'I'd marry you tomorrow if you'd have me, and you know it.'

'Hamish——' Mora looked appealingly at him, not wanting to have their private affairs brought to the table and discussed in this way.

'Of course, my dear Mora.' It was Sir James that came to the rescue again, his bright blue eyes understanding and sympathetic. 'It's no business of anyone else's but you and Hamish. We'll say no more.' No more was said, but Mora knew that the other girl had achieved her object and embarrassed her in front of the family, and she shivered at the look of malice that reached her across the table before the dark eyes were lowered modestly.

Helen Murdoe seemed in no hurry to depart after dinner and to Mora's discomfort she followed her from the house when she went out into the courtyard for a breath of air, feeling that she needed to be on her own and to breathe freely after the uncomfortable experience at dinner.

Short of being outright rude and ignoring her, there was little Mora could do about her unwanted companion and together they walked round the gravelled courtyard in the cold dampness of the night air. They walked in silence for a moment or two, then Helen Murdoe turned her fine eyes to Mora, her expression in the yellow light from the windows curious and wary.

'Did you manage to beat the storm this morning?' she asked, and for the first time Mora realised why she had tried so hard to dissuade her from riding round the loch instead of coming the straight way home. She had known that Adam McLean was out there still, on that path, on his way home, and she had not wanted them to meet. Mora almost laughed out loud at the idea, but a second later felt sorry for the girl that she should need to go to such lengths to keep Adam from seeing any other woman if she possibly could.

'I'm afraid I didn't,' she admitted. 'I should have taken your advice and gone the short way home.'

'You'll have got a real soaking, then?' the soft voice suggested, not without satisfaction, and Mora smiled ruefully.

'Yes, I did, though it could have been worse if I hadn't found shelter in the little hut along there.'

'The shieling,' Helen Murdoe corrected her disdainfully. 'You'll have seen Adam, then?'

'Yes, I did,' Mora admitted. 'And I'm very glad I did, for I'd never have found it on my own.'

The dark eyes narrowed as Helen looked at her in the almost dark. 'Did you not know it was there?'

'No,' Mora confessed. 'I must have been past it several times, but I'd never noticed it, and if Adam hadn't taken me there, I probably never would have.'

'A gallant rescue, no doubt,' the girl said sarcastically, and Mora flushed at her tone.

'As you say,' she said quietly. 'He built a fire and made coffee and I was very glad of both, I was soaking wet and very cold.'

There was a heavy silence for a few seconds while they walked side by side round the gravel perimeter of the courtyard. 'You're here ostensibly to gather material for that book of yours, are you not?' Helen Murdoe asked, and Mora flushed at the implication.

'I *am* getting material for my book, Miss Murdoe,' she answered quietly, though she knew her voice trembled betrayingly. 'I've spent the whole afternoon with Mr. Ian McLean and we've made tremendous progress.'

'Oh, I'm sure you have,' the other agreed. 'Was Adam with his grandfather?'

Tempted as she was to lie, Mora answered truthfully. 'No, he wasn't. Why do you ask?'

'I think you know why I ask,' Helen Murdoe said softly. 'Adam spends a lot of time with his grandfather and so do you, and I'd not like you to get any wrong ideas about Adam McLean, Miss O'Connell.'

'I—I don't think I have,' Mora answered, wishing this

64

embarrassing and distasteful conversation could end. 'Do you mind if we go in now? I'm getting rather cold.' She turned towards the doors and would have moved away, but Helen Murdoe put out a hand and stopped her, her fingers strong and hard as she gripped her arm.

'I'm just giving you a friendly warning, that's all,' she said in her soft voice, her dark eyes glittering in the diffused light from the windows. 'Don't get involved with Adam McLean; he's not free to *get* involved with anyone. Any plans for the future concern me, not you, Miss O'Connell, and I'd like you to remember that.' The chilling menace in the soft quiet voice sent a shiver along Mora's spine as she wrenched her arm free of the restraining grip and ran up the two steps to the door.

CHAPTER FIVE

Try as she would Mora could not rid herself of the uneasiness that Helen Murdoe's warning had stirred in her. She had been appalled at the cold malice in the girl's voice and the hatred she appeared to have for her, wondering how much worse she might have felt if she had known about the visit to the south tower on the night after her arrival at Glen Ghyll and the kiss that Adam McLean had treated so lightly.

There was the added thought too that he might have told Helen Murdoe about that night and, innocent as it had been, the other girl would not treat it as lightly as Adam had done, she had no doubt. She was angry too that he did not openly admit his association with the girl and sometimes could even sympathise with her for feeling so deeply about anyone as irresponsible as he was. Mora saw him more often than she liked, but as it was usually in the company of his grandfather, it should help to dispel any suspicion Helen Murdoe might have.

Hamish saw her less often than he would have liked, although they rode fairly often and walked sometimes, as often as the weather permitted now that the winter was drawing in. She enjoyed walking on her own and often felt guilty when Hamish apologised so profusely for leaving her to her own devices.

It was a lovely clear morning when she decided to leave the castle by the back way, via the stable yard and down the slope towards the stream, or the burn as she was beginning to call it. It was a pleasant walk, particularly when the morning was crisp and clear with the sharpness of frost as it

66

was this morning. Glittering and crackling under foot as she left the yard and approached Rob Smith's small cottage just beyond the stables.

Mrs. Smith, a plumply pretty girl, helped in the castle, cleaning and polishing, and Mora had seen her several times, so that she smiled recognition when she saw her at the door of the cottage. 'It's a nice morning,' Mora called, and the girl nodded.

'It is,' she agreed and, though she smiled, Mora thought she looked a little preoccupied, as if something was worrying her, and she continually watched the path down to the stream.

'Are you looking for someone?' Mora asked, stopping at the gate. 'Perhaps I'll see whoever it is and I can tell them you're waiting.'

'Och, 'tis the laddie,' Mrs. Smith said cautiously. 'There's no tellin' what mischief he's on doon there. I've ta chase him every time, he willna stay in, an' he'll catch his death doon there.'

Mora looked vaguely surprised. 'I didn't know you had a family, Mrs. Smith. I've never seen a child about the place.' She laughed, half apologetically. 'Not that there's any reason I should, of course.'

'He'll be gone ta the burn again,' Mrs. Smith told her. 'Och, he's a wilful one, that lad, he'll no be told it's dangerous sae near the water.'

'I'm going that way,' said Mora. 'Don't you bother coming out in the cold again, I'll send him back home.'

The girl looked uncertain, a look of apprehensive indecision in her eyes, then she shook her head. 'I'll no bother ye, Miss O'Connell, I can bring him back.'

'Nonsense,' Mora laughed. 'It's no bother to me. You stay here, I'm sure you're busy, and I'll send the boy home. What's his name?' she added, and surprised an even warier look on the plump face.

'Oh, ay—Richard. We call him Richie, but——'

'Then I'll send Master Richie packing,' Mora laughed

'don't you worry, Mrs. Smith.'

'Thank you.' As Mora turned away and walked on over the crackling turf she was aware of the wary and vaguely unhappy eyes following her and she wondered what the reason for Effie Smith's reluctance was.

The sun was struggling gamely against threatening clouds as Mora crossed the expanse of wooded grassland heading towards the stream, which was deeper here than in any other part of its course and made Effie Smith's concern for the boy's safety understandable.

She could see a small figure at the very edge of the water, bending over and prodding in the water with a stick and she felt a momentary warmth in her heart at the eternal and simple pleasures of small boys. He either did not hear her approach or he intended to ignore her as a possible interruption of his game, for he made no effort to turn round and she called his name as she came nearer.

'Richie!' The dark head turned reluctantly and a pair of grey eyes looked at her over one shoulder while he continued to make a splash with his stick in the water. He was perhaps five years old, though he could have been younger, and she dreaded to think what could happen if he had fallen into the iciness of the running stream.

'Ice,' he informed her briefly as she joined him. There was no ice on the stream itself, but a puddle at his feet had been shattered into thin slivers that were already melting.

'Only on the puddles,' she said. 'There's none on the stream, and you're getting awfully wet splashing like that, aren't you?'

He paused in his labours and looked down at the front of his long-trousered woollen suit. 'Mm,' he agreed. 'It's wet.' The wide grey eyes looked up at her with an almost adult curiosity and she found their gaze curiously familiar. 'Who are you?' he asked.

The blunt question and the frankness of his curiosity made her smile. 'Mora O'Connell,' she said, 'and I know you're Richie Smith.'

68

He frowned. 'I'm not,' he denied stoutly, 'I'm Richie Gordon.'

'Oh.' She could not hide her surprise and she saw the child's grey eyes studying her with pitying scorn for her mistake. 'I'm sorry, Richie, I thought——'

'Why isn't there ice on the burn?' he asked, and Mora rapidly left the matter of his identity for the more urgent one of why ice had not formed on the water of the stream.

'Because it's running too fast,' she explained. 'It has to be a very hard frost to freeze running water like that.'

'Oh.' He looked as if he doubted her opinion and would have argued the point, but at that moment something behind her caught his eye and his face beamed into delight as he dropped his stick into the water and ran past her. 'Adam! Adam!'

Mora's heart stirred uneasily when she realised the identity of the newcomer and she turned and looked across to where Adam McLean was dismounting from the big black he invariably rode. The boy's little legs moved as fast as they were able and the man stood waiting for him, his arms outstretched, sweeping him off his feet as he reached him, the two of them laughing delightedly. It was several minutes before the man became aware of her beside the stream, or at least until he gave any sign that he saw her.

The deep grey eyes held the familiar hint of challenge as he looked at her and she came across to where he stood with the boy. 'Good morning,' he said, 'did the frost frighten you off riding?'

'No, I just preferred to walk,' she said shortly, resentment as usual making her sound stiffly formal. 'I promised Mrs. Smith I'd send Richie home,' she added, still puzzled over the boy's name. 'I thought he was her son, but he tells me his name's Gordon.'

'Effie Smith only takes care of him,' he told her, and obviously intended enlightening her no further.

'Can I ride with you, Adam?' The boy tugged at his jacket, his eyes pleading, and Mora found it hard to attribute the expression she saw on Adam McLean's face to the man she thought she knew. He put a hand on the boy's dark head and ruffled his hair, a smile on his face as he shook his head slowly, and seemingly with regret.

'Only back as far as Mrs. Smith's,' he told him, 'then I'll have to leave you. I'm meeting someone and I can't take you with me.'

The boy's face fell and his lower lip thrust out in disappointment. 'Why not?' he demanded, and Mora saw the quick frown that flicked across Adam McLean's dark face before he replied.

'I'm meeting Miss Murdoe,' he told him quietly, 'and you don't want to be a nuisance, do you?'

Richie shook his head. 'I don't *like* her,' he said with what was presumably characteristic bluntness. The wide eyes looked at Mora, who was feeling oddly superfluous in this rather personal discussion. 'I like her,' he added, '*she's* all right.'

Mora flushed, not so much at the unexpected compliment, but at the mocking smile it induced from Adam McLean. He was laughing at her again in the way she found most infuriating and she could feel her temper rising as the deep quiet laugh taunted her.

'I'm glad someone approves of me,' she said shortly, and Richie looked puzzled, his wide eyes glancing from one to the other of them.

'Oh, I approve of you,' Adam McLean assured her. 'I very definitely approve of you, but you have got a temper, haven't you, Paddy?'

'I haven't,' she denied crossly. 'At least, not usually I haven't. It's just that—that you bring the worst out in me. I mean,' she amended hastily, 'you always seem to annoy me. Deliberately, I suspect.'

'Never,' he denied, the expression in his eyes giving lie to the seeming sincerity of the protest.

'Adam!' Richie was tired of being ignored and was pulling at Adam's jacket again. '*Are* you going to take me home on Klonda?'

'Right now,' Adam promised him. 'Come along.' He lifted the boy into the saddle, then mounted the big black again himself. 'O.K.?' he queried, and Richie nodded, a wide grin on his face, while Adam looked down at Mora. 'Sorry we can't take you too, Paddy, but even Klonda wouldn't take three of us, and besides, young Richie here is a fidget.' She made no reply, only tried not to colour under the mocking scrutiny of his eyes, and he put his heels to the black with a casual wave of one hand to her as they rode off.

Only once before had Hamish taken her out to dinner in Cairndale and it was by way of being a treat, although Mora always found mealtimes at the castle very enjoyable and had no hankerings after the bright lights of town. Not that Cairndale was a large town, but it was fairly thriving one, thanks mainly to the McLean business which provided employment for most of the male inhabitants and some of the women.

There was one good restaurant whose cuisine was excellently served but homely, and Mora enjoyed the change, even the chance of talking to Hamish alone, although she knew it meant the inevitable proposal when dinner was finished.

'You look lovely,' he told her as they sat over coffee. 'I've never seen you looking lovelier. Our Scottish air suits you.'

Mora laughed softly, the wine they had taken, lending an added sparkle to her deep blue eyes. 'It does suit me,' she agreed. 'I feel as if I belong here somehow. I love it.'

'I'm glad.' He leaned across the table towards her, his grey eyes earnest and sincere as he looked at her. 'I hope you'll be staying, Mora, for ever. Will you?'

She shook her head, hating to reject him yet again. 'I don't think so, Hamish, I really don't. And please,' she put a hand on his arm her eyes pleading, 'don't be hurt. I—I think perhaps it would be best if I left Glen Ghyll.'

71

'Leave?' He stared at her in dismay. 'You can't, Mora, you can't leave so soon!'

She smiled and shook her head, speaking slowly, choosing her words carefully. 'I've been here almost a month now, Hamish, and I think your family expect—well, they expect us to become engaged, don't they? It's the prime reason they've all been so—so nice to me, accepted me so willingly into their home. I'm beginning to feel that I'm there under false pretences. Although I've told everyone that I'm researching for my book, I don't think any of them really believe it.'

'They all like you very much,' he said, a dark unhappiness in his eyes as he studied her face.

'I know,' she said softly, 'but because they're thinking of me as a prospective member of the family, that's the main reason. They think of me as one of the family, or as someone soon to be one of the family, not as a stranger merely there to dig into their history.'

'And you won't marry me?' His eyes had a remarkable similarity to the boy, Richie, when he pleaded with her and she found herself wondering again about the boy and his friendship with Adam McLean. Some time, she thought, she would ask Hamish about Richie Gordon, but now was not the right time. Also some instinctive warning told her that she would not like the answer he gave.

Meanwhile his proposal was the immediate problem. 'I can't marry you, Hamish, not feeling as I do,' she said. 'It wouldn't be fair to either of us, you must see that.' She shook her head, her eyes pleading for understanding. 'That's why I think it best that I leave Glen Ghyll, now, before things get too involved and your family wonder why—well, why our relationship isn't put on a more permanent basis.'

'Back to London?' he asked gloomily, and she nodded. 'But do you have to? I mean, you have your own place in London, so why not here?'

'Here?' She frowned curiously, her heart fluttering hopefully at the prospect of a way out for her other than having to leave the old castle and the family she had become quite fond of in the time she had known them. 'I don't see how I could, Hamish.'

'Of course you could,' Hamish insisted, encouraged by her hesitation. 'There's plenty of room, God knows. You could have a room at Glen Ghyll as easily as anywhere else, couldn't you? *And* you'd be right here where you can go on with your research.'

Mora hesitated still. It was a temptation and she thought she would not be able to resist it. The thought of going back to London after the grandeur of Castle Glen Ghyll was not a pleasing one, there would be so much she would miss.

'But—could I? I mean,' she added hastily, 'would Sir James consent to such an arrangement?'

'Father? Of course he would. He likes you and he never minds how many people there are in the place. He's a gregarious creature, unlike me.' He looked at her hopefully. 'Shall I put it to him?'

'As a straightforward arrangement—renting a room, just as if it was anywhere else?' He nodded. 'I—I don't know. I would like to stay on, in fact I'd love to, but it does seem rather as if I'm imposing on your family.'

'Nonsense, of course you're not. If that's the way you want it, no one will question it.' That was unlikely, Mora thought, though the questions would not be directed at her but at Hamish, in her absence, and she wondered what explanations he would give.

'I'd like to very much,' she said, 'but there is one thing, Hamish. It would have to be clearly understood that I was not there as your—your——'

'My fiancée?' He smiled wryly over the word. 'No, I understand that, and at least you'll be under the same roof. While you're at Glen Ghyll I can hope, can't I?'

'I can hardly stop you doing that,' she agreed. 'I'm sorry, Hamish.' She covered his clenched hands as they lay on the table either side of an empty coffee cup. 'I do *like* you enormously, but I don't love you and I can't marry you unless I do. You understand, don't you?'

He nodded, but did not look at her, his face blank and distant. 'I understand,' he said quietly, and she shivered as if there was some hidden meaning behind the words.

They drove home almost in silence, with a few light flakes of snow fluttering in the headlights along the narrow bumpy road, so that Mora wondered if she had done the right thing in deciding to stay on at Glen Ghyll if they were to be snowed in for any length of time.

They turned into the wide, tree-lined drive and the snow was falling thicker now so that the figure that stepped out from the deep stone archway was almost invisible even in the headlights and Mora was reminded of the first time she arrived at Glen Ghyll. Of the fleeting glimpse she had had of a dark face in the shadowed depth of the archway and which she had, until now, forgotten.

Snow sprinkled the dark hair and clung to his eyelashes and when Hamish braked and wound down the window, an impatient frown on his face, he put his head inside the car. 'Have you seen anything of Doctor Lowrie on the road?' he asked, none of the usual lightness and mockery in the deep voice, only anxiety and a trace of impatience.

'Doctor Lowrie? No, we haven't.' Hamish looked at his brother anxiously. 'Is it Tizzy?' he asked, and Adam shook his head.

'No,' he said shortly, 'it's Grandfather.'

Hamish stared at him for a moment uncomprehendingly. 'Grandfather? But—but he was all right when I saw him last.'

'Which was two days ago,' Adam reminded him shortly. His eyes went to Mora, her face drawn and anxious at the news. She had become extremely fond of the old man in the weeks she had been there. 'He'd like to see you, Mora, if you would.' It was the first time she had seen those deep, arrogant eyes pleading and she felt a prick of tears as she

74

nodded her head.

'Of course,' she said, her voice husky. 'I'll go right away.'

'Good. Thank you.' The dark, snow-spattered head withdrew and Hamish wound up the window again without a word. There had been no request for Hamish to visit his grandfather, she noticed, and the thought left her sad but not really surprised.

She turned at the foot of the stairs and looked at Hamish's unhappy face. 'You should come with me,' she urged softly. 'You should, Hamish, you're his grandson.'

The grey eyes looked at her for a moment and she thought he would do as she asked, but then his pride overcame compassion and he shook his head. 'No,' he told her. 'You go, it's you he's asked for.' And he turned on his heel and went across the hall to the big room, his shoes leaving a wet pattern across the carpet.

Ramsey admitted her to Ian McLean's bedroom with a finger raised warningly to his lips. 'He's no sae guid,' he whispered, his small dark eyes suspiciously bright as he followed her to the bedside. 'He'll mebbe no see ye sae weil either, lassie.'

Mora was shocked at the change in the old man since only that morning, when she drew closer to the bed and looked down at the face on the pillow. Always frail and delicate-looking, the thin features looked like those of a very old man and her heart thudded dismayingly hard against her ribs as she took the thin hands gently in hers.

'Mora?' The blue eyes opened wearily and looked at her, a flutter of smile round his mouth. 'Mora.'

'Yes,' she said softly, bending nearer for fear he might not hear her. 'Adam said you wanted to see me, Grandfather McLean, so here I am.'

'Ah, yes.' He sounded as if every word required tremendous effort and his voice was a thin parody of his usual brusque tone. 'You came.' This, for the moment, seemed to content him and he lay with his eyes closed, his breathing shallow and uneven while Ramsey stood, anxious-eyed, at the foot of the bed. It seemed so silent in the room that Mora felt a tremor of fear, as if the old man had already left them and, as though he sensed her fear, Ian McLean opened his eyes again. 'When—when are you going to—to marry my grandson?' he whispered, and for a moment the blue eyes were fixed on her almost as brightly as of old and she smiled, though she wished he had asked her anything but that.

'I don't know,' she said softly. 'It's—it's not a thing one should rush into, is it? I must be sure.'

'Of course you must, my dear.' The thin fingers stirred under her hand and she moved them gently. 'But you *will* marry him, won't you? He loves you, you know, he loves you very much—I know, I can see it in his eyes.'

'I know he does,' Mora said gently, 'but I can't make such a promise, Grandfather McLean. Not about marriage, it would mean too much to me to marry for any other reason than because I loved him too. You do see that, don't you?'

'Yes, yes, of course.' The thin voice sounded unutterably weary.

'I think you should try and sleep now,' she told him. 'Doctor Lowrie is on his way and he won't be very pleased with me if I sit here talking to you when you should be sleeping, will he?'

He shook his head, a slow weary gesture that brought a lump to her throat and threatened to send tears rolling down her cheeks. 'I don't want to sleep,' he said. 'Not just yet.' Mora had no time to answer before the door behind her opened to admit Adam and a tall, heavily built man with red hair who smelled of wet tweed and disinfectant.

Mora rose from the edge of the bed and gently disengaged her hands from the old man's, looking at the doctor anxiously as she passed him. Adam gave her a grateful half smile as he opened the door for her.

'Thank you,' he whispered as she walked past him and

she turned wide, troubled eyes to him. 'I'll see you later if I may,' he added with uncharacteristic humility, and she nodded silently.

She went to her own room and took off the topcoat she still wore, discarding too her gaily-coloured dress, with a sudden revulsion for its brightness. She donned a more sober dark green one and went downstairs, wondering what effect the old man's sudden turn for the worse would have had on his family.

Hamish came across the room to her, his eyes consoling her, his hands gentle as he took her arm, as if he understood her feelings and was in sympathy with them. 'I'm sorry about that, Mora. Sorry you had to be plunged into our affairs so suddenly. How is the old man?' he added.

'He's very ill,' she said, her voice husky with suppressed emotion. 'He's very ill indeed, Hamish, and he looks so—so forlorn somehow. Forsaken.' The word came, unbidden, and Sir James, overhearing it, looked up sharply, his blue eyes narrowed as if he suspected criticism.

'My father chooses to be alone, Mora. He's never wanted the family round him, ever.'

'Oh, I didn't intend it as a criticism,' Mora said hastily. 'It's just that—it was just the impression he gave me.' For the first time Mora realised that Helen Murdoe was in the room and she felt the wide, beautiful eyes watching her intently from the other side of the fireplace.

'Adam's with the old man, isn't he?' Fergus asked, and Mora nodded.

'Adam and Doctor Lowrie.'

Alison McLean snorted impatiently, a frown ageing her sharp features. 'You should be up there with Father, James,' she told her brother. 'You have more right to be there than Adam has.'

Sir James merely frowned at the suggestion and reached for a decanter to fill his glass. 'I'm not wanted up there,' he said shortly. 'Let Adam have his day while he can.' There was an ominous ring to the words and Mora wondered what undercurrents of dislike and even hate ran beneath the cosy family exterior of the McLeans. Adam was the self-confessed black sheep, but she had yet to discover the reason for his disgrace and his unpopularity with the rest of the family, apart from his arrogance and disregard for conventional behaviour.

It was much later than usual when Mora retired to her room and she had scarcely closed the door when she thought she heard movement at the top of the stairs. If someone was coming from the north wing she would like to know how the old man was and she opened the door again and looked out.

Adam McLean was about to descend and, hearing her, he turned and came back, his eyes lacking their usual glitter of mockery, deeper and tired-looking. 'How—how is he?' Mora asked anxiously, dreading the answer.

'He's alive,' said Adam, painfully blunt, 'and that's about all one can say.' He looked at her for a moment in silence, some unbearable emotion flicking a succession of expressions across the mobile face. 'Talk to me, Mora. For a little while—just talk to me, will you?'

She swallowed hard on the constriction in her throat and nodded, closing the bedroom door behind her and turning instinctively towards the south wing. 'The south tower?' she asked, and he led the way without question, his long stride moderated to allow her to keep pace with him.

It was windy and cold on the square, stone tower and darker than the last time they had come up here, the moon not yet risen. He helped her up the narrow stairs, then crossed to the wall and stood looking down at the barely discernible ground below. Neither of them spoke for some time, and Mora, standing beside him, sensed him gradually relax and become less tense. She realised too that she had been silly not to put on a coat, but the invitation had been so unexpected and so urgent that it had not even entered her head. The east wind ruffled her hair and blew it about her face and neck, and she shivered involuntarily when it chilled her to the bone through the fine woollen dress she wore.

Adam turned to her, his features indistinguishable in the darkness, his voice unusually contrite when he spoke. 'You're cold,' he said. 'I'm sorry, Mora, I'm a selfish devil, I should have realised you hadn't a coat.' He was taking off his thick tweed jacket as he spoke and she started to protest.

'There's no need——'

'It will help,' he interrupted. 'Though it's little enough in this wind.' He put the jacket round her shoulders and she shrugged gratefully into the warmth of it. 'Is that better?'

'Much better, thank you, but what about you?' She saw a smile flick briefly across his face, a glimpse of white teeth in the darkness. His hands still held the jacket round her and she could feel the incredible warmth of him as he pulled her closer.

'Don't worry about me,' he said. 'I'm tough.' She remembered his request that she should talk to him, and the way he had looked, and she doubted the complete truth of that assertion. The desperate loneliness of his plea had touched her heart and she had followed him without a second thought. Only now, as they stood on the wind-chilled darkness of the ancient tower, did she realise the impulsiveness of her action and debate the wisdom of it.

'Just the same,' she said, trying to sound matter-of-fact, 'you could catch a chill in this wind with no coat on.'

'And so could you,' he countered with a hint of his more usual lightness, 'so what do you propose we do? Share it?' She did not answer and he was close enough now to lay his face briefly against her wind-ruffled hair. 'You'd better not mention this to Hamish,' he warned her softly, 'or I'll be a blacker sheep than ever in his eyes.'

Mora stirred uneasily at the reminder and raised her eyes, though she could scarcely see him. 'You'd better not tell Helen Murdoe either,' she retorted, 'or I'll be thought even worse of, too.' She heard the dry chuckle he gave and felt his fingers twine into the curls on her neck, gently tugging as if to reprimand her.

'You'd have a long way to go to catch me,' he told her. 'And neither Hamish nor Helen are such paragons of virtue either if it comes down to it.' This was her chance, she realised, to discover what the reason was for Hamish's uneasiness in Helen Murdoe's company, and she hesitated only briefly before voicing her curiosity.

'What makes Hamish so—so uneasy whenever Miss Murdoe is here?' she asked, and wondered, when he was silent for so long, if she had overstepped the boundaries of discretion, but she did not think he was angry, for his hands were no less gentle as he held her and his voice, when he *did* answer was only cautious.

'You should ask Hamish that, really,' he said. 'But I suppose there's no harm in my telling you. He was once engaged to Helen, but—it was broken off.'

'I see.' She did not know whether the news surprised her or not, but it did explain Hamish's discomfiture in the other girl's presence and it needed no special clairvoyance on anyone's part to guess who had been the reason for the broken engagement. It would explain too, the old man's frequent sly illusions to the McLean men coveting each other's women, but it did not explain why Adam was regarded as the black sheep and was more or less ostracised by his family while Helen Murdoe seemed to be still acceptable to them.

Why he had not married the girl or even become engaged to her she did not try to reason, and Helen Murdoe had no ring on her left hand. They were scarcely things she could ask him about.

His quiet chuckle brought her out of her reverie and he held her away from him, looking down at her, trying to see her face in the darkness. 'And you have no doubt who was responsible for the break, have you?'

'I didn't——' she began.

'Poor Paddy,' he teased her softly, 'so many questions

80

and so few answers!' She would have protested or at least disclaimed her right to any answers, but he bent his head and his mouth held her silent for a long delirious minute until she stirred protestingly and stepped back against the coldness of the stone wall.

'We'd better go,' she whispered, and noted with dismay the way her voice trembled. 'It's getting cold up here.' It was less than the truth, for in fact she felt warmly glowing from head to toe as she moved towards the dark doorway into the tower room, and she wondered if the ghosts of Marjorie Stewart McLean and her illicit lover smiled in the dark corners of the bare cold room, to see their story repeated.

CHAPTER SIX

SURPRISINGLY, to Mora at least, the old man survived the night, and the pale sun that shone in through the high windows next morning seemed like an omen to her as she bathed and dressed ready for breakfast. She stood before the mirror in her room, brushing her dark hair until it shone and curled softly, her eyes thoughtful, wondering if her prayers would be answered and that Ian McLean would be spared for a few more years at least. Realising, too, that it was her own fear of loss that prompted the wish, for the old man must surely have endured enough pain during the past few years to make the end almost welcome.

Across the expanse of garden below her window she saw two figures approaching and stopped her vigorous brushing to watch them, frowning curiously. One of them was Adam McLean, neatly dressed in a dark suit as she had seen him only once before, and the other was the tiny, stocky figure of the boy, Richie Gordon, his short legs trying to match his companion's pace, though it was considerably slower than usual.

Adam's left hand was on the boy's shoulder and every so often she saw the child look up at him curiously, while Adam responded with a reassuring smile. The two of them finally disappeared across the cobbled yard by the stables and presumably under the rear archway into the castle.

Mora frowned curiously, putting down the hairbrush and giving a last absent-minded smooth to her dress before going downstairs. She had one hand on the door handle, ready to leave, when she heard raised voices on the stairs and hesitated to step into what could prove to be a family quarrel.

She heard Hamish's voice, coldly angry, and Adam's deeper and quieter, both wordless with the thickness of the stone walls to muffle them, but telling enough in tone alone.

Footsteps sounded again on the uncarpeted treads of the staircase and she ventured to open her door. Adam and the boy were walking away from her down the northern end of the corridor and Hamish was out of sight down the stairs within a second of her appearance. Neither of them were aware of her proximity, she felt sure, or Adam at least would have turned and acknowledged her. That she attributed the less boorish manner to Adam and not to Hamish did not strike her as strange at all.

She left her room and walked the short distance to the stairs and Hamish was already turning the corner towards the breakfast room, the ramrod stiffness of his back telling its own story.

Fergus was already seated at the table when she opened the door and Hamish stood by one of the chairs his hands clenched on the curved back of it, his face black with an anger she had never seen there before.

'He has no right!' he declared as Mora opened the door, and she saw Fergus hastily send him a warning with his eyes. When he turned there was a tight smile round his mouth, but his eyes still blazed angrily.

'Good morning, Mora, did you manage to get some sleep?'

'A little,' Mora admitted, aware of the atmosphere of tension in the little room. 'How is Grandfather McLean this morning, have you heard?'

'About the same.' It was Fergus who answered her, seeming in better control of himself than his brother. 'He's no better and I don't suppose he ever will be now.' There was a horrible finality about the words and the way they were spoken, and Mora felt herself chill with the inevitability of it.

'I'm sorry.' Her regret was plain in her voice and she wondered if her own grief at Ian McLean's condition was not more deep than his grandsons' or even his son's. They had never made any pretence of being fond of the old man and she did not think them sufficiently false-faced to pretend otherwise now. Only Adam had ever admitted to caring deeply about the old man.

'You're quite attached to Grandfather, aren't you?' It was Hamish who asked, his voice more normally steady now, and Mora nodded. Hamish smiled wryly at her; though his eyes were still darkly angry. 'It's because you're so lovely,' he told her. 'Grandfather McLean could never resist a pretty girl, and they seem to like him too. I think the old rascal revelled in the fact.' Uneasily Mora remembered the old man's embarrassing question of the night before and she bit her lip when she recalled her own noncommittal answer.

'I liked him,' she said simply, without realising she had used the past tense.

It was only an hour later that the door of the big room opened and Adam stood in the doorway, his deep grey eyes dark with some unbearable hurt, his hand on the shoulder of the boy, Richie. 'Grandfather would like to see you,' he said, his voice even deeper than usual, 'all of you.' He looked at Mora. 'Mora, would you take Richie home, please? I can't leave now and I—we don't want him here when——' He stopped and she saw his fingers tighten on the boy's shoulder, the knuckles showing white.

'Of course I'll take him,' Mora said softly, and thought Hamish would have protested, but thought better of it. 'Come along, Richie.'

The boy went without a murmur and with only a brief puzzled glance at Adam before he left the circle of eyes that watched him with mixed expressions.

It was snowing and an east wind sent flurries of white

84

swirling round every corner. Mora had said she would leave at once, but Sir James would not hear of it and he persuaded her to stay. He was quite charming about it and seemed older, suddenly, at the death of his father, though there was little pretence at overwhelming grief among the family and only Tizzy shed tears for him. Miss Alison McLean remained firmly in command of her emotions, and if she felt any sense of loss, she concealed it very well.

Mora could scarcely believe that Ian McLean had gone, that she would no more visit the room in the north wing, or spend hours talking to the old man and laughing with him as she had done during the last month, under the watchful but indulgent eye of Ramsey, the manservant. What would happen to Ramsey, she had no idea, but she could not imagine him fitting into the household downstairs, since he looked upon the rest of the family with a jaundiced eye. All save Adam, of course; he approved of Adam because the old man had and because the two of them had spent so much time together; for the same reason he liked Mora and made no pretence of hiding it.

The family vault in the tiny churchyard at Glencairn had received Ian McLean amid a flurry of falling snow, and Mora was surprised at the number of people who attended. Apparently the old man had been a very popular figure before his accident, and most of the village and the workers from the surrounding crofts had braved the storm to pay their last respects.

Mora had noticed Helen Murdoe among the invited mourners, accompanied by an elderly woman, presumably her mother, and several times the girl's eyes had been watching her whenever she glanced up, narrowed and malicious, as if she resented her presence there.

Adam McLean, she noticed, did not stand with the rest of his family, but beside Helen Murdoe and her mother, his dark head bowed, flecked with the whiteness of snow so that he looked older and more severe than she had ever seen him. He looked at no one across the few feet that separated him from his family and spoke only a word or two to Helen Murdoe.

Afterwards, when the snow had eased and the mourners paused to say their last goodbyes, Mora was aware of Helen Murdoe at her elbow and the soft voice speaking, words meant for her ears alone. 'I'm surprised to see you still here, Miss O'Connell. I wouldn't have thought strangers welcome at a time like this.'

Mora turned and looked at the gauntly attractive face, with its lovely eyes and perfect complexion, and saw it only vaguely through a haze of tears. 'Mr. McLean was a very good friend,' she said quietly, her voice husky with emotion. 'I shall miss him a lot.'

'No doubt,' Helen Murdoe said dryly. 'But you'll probably find things are a little different at Glen Ghyll now that the old man's gone. You may not be as welcome as you were.'

'I was quite ready to leave,' Mora said, 'but Sir James asked me to stay on.'

'Did he?' The fine brows arched in surprise. 'No doubt under the impression that you and Hamish are——' She spread her hands and shrugged expressively. 'But *are* you?'

Mora flushed, partly in anger and partly embarrassment. It could not possibly concern this girl how she and Hamish felt about each other, nor whether they intended to marry or not, and this was certainly neither the time nor the place to mention it. 'I don't think this is the time to discuss my relationship with Hamish, Miss Murdoe,' she said. 'And if you'll forgive my saying so, I don't quite see how it concerns you in any way.'

Anger lent an almost primitive beauty to the fine-boned face and the dark eyes flashed and sparkled with fury as she faced Mora. 'It concerns me that you're living so close to Adam McLean,' she told her, her soft voice chill as ice and barely more than a whisper. 'If you intend marrying Hamish I advise you to do so, if not I suggest you leave Glen

86

Ghyll before things become too uncomfortable for you. I've known the McLeans all my life and I've no intention of letting some little upstart, claiming to be a relation, upset my plans!'

Mora stared at her for a moment, appalled by the malice that was directed at her. 'I—don't know what plans you have,' she said, 'and I certainly have no idea how I could upset them.'

'No? Well, I suggest you leave, Miss O'Connell. Leave right now and go back to London where you belong.' They both saw Adam at that moment, coming across towards them, and Mora thanked heaven, for feeling as she was, she found the girl's spite almost unbearable and she was not far off making a complete fool of herself by crying like a child. She felt suddenly very small and vulnerable and in need of Hamish's comforting arm.

'Excuse me,' she whispered, her throat constricted and dry so that she choked on the words.

Hamish turned round as she approached and, seeing her pale-faced and tearful, hastened to her, pulling her into the curve of his arm and resting his face briefly against her forehead. 'I wondered where you were, my dear,' he said softly. 'I forgot for a moment how fond you were of Grandfather McLean.' His sympathy, though comforting and welcome, was almost too much for her self-control and she merely nodded her head as he helped her into the car. Miss Alison McLean frowned her disapproval of such a display of weakness and sat stiffly upright, her fierce blue eyes missing nothing.

During the next three weeks Mora gave all her attention to her book. Putting into some semblance of order all the information that old Ian McLean had given her over the weeks, she found the work helped to ease the unhappiness she felt at his passing.

She had seen Adam McLean several times when she had ventured out for walks, braving the snow that still lay and the east winds that cut like knives through even the thickest clothing. He seemed quieter now, less given to sudden and insolent laughter, but he still had that same arrogant manner towards her and they had quarrelled once about her taking out Mist for a ride when he had decreed that it was unsafe for her to do so. It had, inevitably, been she who had given in eventually and retreated under the mocking gaze of the deep grey eyes, but she thought his anger was more intense now and less teasing.

He still came to the castle sometimes as he had when the old man had been alive, only now she noticed that he joined the others, Fergus, Hamish and his father, in the room that served as a study for Sir James, and where most of the family business affairs were discussed. His presence at the meetings surprised her, for he had never before attended them and she was under the impression that he had no connection with the firm at all.

It was from this room that Mora heard angry voices one morning as she came downstairs from her room. The words were indistinguishable, but there was no mistaking the angry tone of the voices, and she wondered what new quarrel had divided the family.

The door opened suddenly and Hamish came out into the hall, his expression thunderous, his grey eyes dark with temper. Seeing her, he paused, attempting a smile which failed dismally. 'Come for a walk with me,' he suggested abruptly. 'I need some air and at least the sun's shining out there.'

Mora glanced at the closed door of the study. 'I thought I heard you—I mean I couldn't help hearing voices raised.' She put a hand on his arm. 'I'm sorry, Hamish.'

'Why should you be?' he asked shortly.

'Because I—I hate to hear you quarrelling like that. It seems so awful when a family is as divided as yours seems to be.'

'It's scarcely what you would call divided,' he said, 'at least not evenly, with only Adam on one side and the rest of us on the other.' His eyes glittered angrily, making him look far more like the brother he despised than he realised. 'We should have expected the old man to do something like that and he did it,' he added. 'Well, as far as I'm concerned Ian McLean and Son can go bankrupt for all I care.'

'Don't, Hamish,' she pleaded. 'Please don't talk like that, you know you don't mean it. The business means too much to you for you to mean it.'

He studied her for a moment in silence, then he pulled her into his arms and buried his face in her soft hair, his fingers tight around her arms. 'You're right, Mora. Of course you're right. I'd work like blazes to keep the firm going and Adam knows it, damn him!'

'Adam?' She raised her head and looked at him curiously. 'Why Adam? He's not connected with the firm, is he?'

Hamish laughed shortly. 'He wasn't,' he said dryly, 'but Grandfather McLean, in his wisdom, left him the majority holding in the firm. He now has fifty-two per cent of the shares!'

'Oh, I see.' She could imagine the old man chuckling with glee at the thought of what disruption and dismay his legacy would cause his family and, much as she had liked him, she could sympathise with Sir James and his other two sons when they learned that the black sheep of the family now held the whip hand. 'It seems a bit unfair,' she added, 'after the three of you have been more or less running the business for the past few years.' She glanced up at him from under her lashes. 'How did Adam take it?'

Hamish laughed shortly. 'How do you think he took it? He's cock-a-hoop now. Getting his own back.' The phrase, she thought, was an odd choice.

'Getting his own back for what?' she asked, and saw the blank, withdrawn look that hid the expression in his eyes.

'Oh, nothing,' he said. 'Just a minor family tiff, nothing you need worry about.' He hugged her close for a moment. 'How about that walk?' he asked. 'I really do need some air.' Obviously he was not as ready as Adam had been to let her know about his former relationship with Helen Murdoe, and she felt a little disappointed that he should have been so reticent about it, when he professed himself in love with her.

'Give me time to fetch a coat,' she said, 'and we'll go.'

'Sorry.' Adam McLean's voice spoke from just behind her. 'We need you back in there, Hamish—if you can be spared, of course.'

The jibe was as much for her as for his brother and she flushed, thinking for a moment that Hamish would hit out, he looked so angry, but instead he bent and kissed Mora's forehead gently and shook his head. 'I'm sorry, my dear, let's make it later, shall we?'

Mora nodded, her cheeks flushed and warm under the scrutiny of Adam's mocking gaze. 'Of course I don't mind,' she told Hamish. 'Later will do just as well.' He glanced angrily at his brother and strode off back towards the study.

'Sorry to break up the party,' Adam said, blandly self-confident. 'But the path of true love—hmm?'

'Nothing of the sort,' she retorted without thinking, and saw his brows rise expressively.

'Oh?' He turned and watched his brother's retreating back briefly. 'My mistake, I rather thought that brother Hamish was captivated.' He studied her face for a few seconds thoughtfully. 'I still think he is, but it has to work both ways, doesn't it?'

'It doesn't concern you,' Mora retorted uneasily, suspecting that he knew how things stood between her and Hamish. 'And I thought you had some urgent business to attend to.' She would have turned away and left him, but his hand on her arm stayed her.

'Mora——' She raised her eyes curiously and looked at him. He gazed at her for a moment, her face flushed and uncertain, her deep blue eyes with their fringe of dark lashes uneasy and hastily lowered. 'Never mind now,' he

90

said with something of the old mockery. 'I'll see you later.'
She watched him go across the hall, hating the self-confident stride and the arrogance of the dark head, but wondering at the rapid beat of her heart and the strange breathlessness she felt. Nothing, she thought, would ever change Adam McLean for very long.

She often walked down in the direction of the stream at the back of the castle, though it was not always easy walking with the snow on the ground and Hamish sought to discourage her, but in vain. She loved the view from that side, of distant snow-covered hills and the restless flow of grey water as it chattered over icy stones in the stream, overhung with branches heavy with snow and almost fairy-like as they glittered in the pale sun, sending showers of powdery white into the water. There was something ageless and incredibly beautiful about it and she never grew tired of looking at it, nor ever thought she would.

The snow was wet now and in places too deep to walk, but the path down to the stream was almost clear and plainly visible. She passed Rob Smith's cottage and caught sight of Effie Smith near the window, waving a hand in greeting. A second later the boy, Richie, appeared at the window, his small face hopeful as he looked out at her, turning to say something to Effie Smith, who shook her head. The boy's face fell and he turned back disconsolately to the window, his lower lip dropped as she had seen it before when he had been disappointed. What his request had been, she could only guess, but his disappointment touched her heart and she made signs to Effie Smith through the window to ask if he could accompany her on her walk.

The girl looked dubious, but must have had second thoughts, for a moment later she appeared at the door of the cottage with Richie in hopeful attendance. 'Would Richie like to come with me?' Mora asked. 'With your permission, of course, Mrs. Smith. I'm not going far only as far as the stream—er—burn and back.'

91

'He's awfu' tired o' bein' cooped up in the house,' Effie Smith said, 'but I'm no sae sure I should——' A small hand tugged at her skirt and the grey eyes appealed irresistibly. 'Aye weil, if ye dinnae mind ta be mithered wi' him, Miss O'Connell, the walk wid mebbe do him guid.'

'I'm sure it would,' Mora agreed, while Richie beamed his delight and hurried away, presumably to fetch warm outdoor clothes.

Suitably muffled against the cold, he joined Mora only minutes later, his wide eyes shining gleefully at being allowed out once more. 'The burn,' he said, running on ahead of her. 'You said the burn, didn't you? You did say the burn?'

'I did,' Mora agreed, smiling at his enthusiasm. 'But I don't propose running all the way there, so you'd better come back and wait for me. There's plenty of time.'

'Will it have ice on?' he asked, obediently rejoining her, his cheeks already glowing in the sharp wind, and Mora shook her head.

'I shouldn't think so,' she told him. 'It's not really cold enough for that.'

He digested the disappointing news in silence for a moment, then the wide curious eyes looked up at her searchingly. 'You live at the castle, don't you?' he asked.

'I'm staying there for a while,' Mora admitted. 'I don't really live there.'

'Like a holiday?' Mora nodded. 'It's nice,' he added wistfully.

'It is nice,' she agreed, 'and very big too.'

He walked on, silent again for a few moments, his expression thoughtful. 'You know G'anfarfer McLean, don't you?' he asked, and she felt that her popularity depended on her answer.

'Yes,' she admitted quietly, 'I knew Grandfather McLean. I liked him very much.'

'He's nice,' he opined, apparently not noticing the discrepancy in tense, and she smiled at the solemn little face passing judgment. 'He said I was—I was—kid it to him,' he informed her confoundingly, and she puzzled over his meaning, wondering what old Ian McLean had said to the boy and if the day of his death was the first time they had met. She had a feeling it was not.

'He likes me,' Richie went on. 'Adam said so.' She remembered the day the old man had died and the circle of curious and unfriendly eyes that had watched Richie leave with her and her voice was gentle when she answered.

'I'm sure he did, Richie. I like you too.'

'Do you?' he asked, and there was something oddly adult and curiously familiar about the way the grey eyes regarded her—a look she had noticed before. 'I'm glad, 'cause I like you too, so does Adam.'

She felt the colour warm her cheeks and laughed uneasily. 'I'm not so sure about that,' she told him. 'But I'm glad *we're* friends, Richie.'

Their arrival at the stream put an end to the conversation and Mora had to admit to relief, for she found the subject of Adam McLean discomfiting and Richie was embarrassingly frank.

She watched him for a while, pushing drifted snow into the water and doing the thousand and one things that small boys find intensely absorbing, and wondered yet again who he was. From his mode of speech he came from a different stratum of life from Effie Smith, who took care of him, and there was a strangely adult air of confidence about him that only seemed to make him more appealing, when in a lot of children it would have been unattractive.

She smiled indulgently as he went about the serious business of attempting to dam the stream with stones and packed snow, quite dry in his long wellington boots. So absorbed was she in watching him and in her own thoughts that she failed to see or hear the approach of a third person and started almost guiltily when Adam McLean appeared at her elbow.

'Perseverance,' he said, and laughed as the flimsy dam

was washed away yet again by the swift flow of the water. Hearing his voice, Richie left his unrewarding task and came over to join them, his rosy face beaming delight at Adam's arrival.

'It won't stay,' he informed him. '*You* build it, Adam.'

'I'm no dam-builder,' Adam objected laughingly, and hastened to explain when he saw the boy's surprised expression. 'I mean I'm no builder of dams, Richie. That's a dam that you were trying to build there.'

'Oh, a dam, dam, dam!' He repeated it with relish until Adam tapped him on the top of his head in warning.

'All right, Richie, now you know, don't drive us mad with it.' He had said nothing to Mora since that first cryptic word, and she again felt like an interloper as she had before when these two had been together. There was a strange rapport between them that struck her as unusual.

'Mora can't build dams,' Richie announced, and his use of her christian name startled her for a moment so that Adam, sensing her surprise, reprimanded the boy, but mildly.

'I don't think Miss O'Connell has give you permission to use her first name, has she?' he asked, and Richie frowned.

'No,' he admitted.

'Then,' Adam said quietly, 'I suggest you wait until she does before you use it again. Right?'

The boy's wide grey eyes looked at her hopefully and she could imagine the difficulty he would have getting his tongue round her much longer surname. 'You can call me Mora by all means, Richie, I don't mind.' Richie gave Adam a look of satisfaction that should have put him firmly in his place, and the man's deep grey eyes laughed at her mockingly.

'How to make friends and influence people,' he grinned. 'You've made another conquest, Paddy. That makes just about everybody so far, doesn't it?'

'Not everybody,' she denied, and he arched a querying brow.

'Oh? Who's the exception? I hope you're not hinting at me, *I'm* definitely conquered.' She was sure the compliment was paid with the express purpose of embarrassing her and she glared at him angrily, glad that Richie had returned to his dam building and could not overhear them.

'I *don't* mean you,' she said crossly, 'and I wish you wouldn't put every conversation on to such a personal basis.' It was difficult whenever she was with him, not to remember the night before old Ian had died and how intimate the conversation had become then—and not only the conversation. She found that whenever Hamish kissed her now, her mind automatically recalled the way Adam had kissed her that night and her own brief surrender to the excitement of it. She was angry with herself for feeling as she did and, rather unfairly, blamed him.

His laugh angered her further. 'Then you can only mean Helen,' he told her. 'Do you?'

Mora bit her lip, unwilling to be involved with him in a discussion concerning Helen Murdoe. 'Since you insist on pursuing the subject—yes, I do mean Miss Murdoe.'

He looked more sober suddenly and a frown drew his brows together. 'I had a feeling you two didn't hit it off,' he said. 'Has she been very catty to you?'

Mora hesitated to answer. 'Oh, I know what Helen can be like,' he added with a wry smile. 'I wondered if you'd caught the sharp edge of her tongue.'

'I think Miss Murdoe is labouring under a—I think she has some mistaken ideas about me.' She chose her words carefully and wished he would not watch her with that embarrassingly intent gaze. 'I can't think why she should have such ideas, but I don't seem able to convince her how wrong she is.'

He seemed to have no doubt what it was Helen Murdoe suspected her of, for he asked for no explanation. 'Have you tried to convince her how wrong she is?' he asked, and she realised with a start that she never had. Never once had she protested to the girl that she had absolutely no reason to be jealous of her own relationship with Adam McLean. She flushed uneasily, kicking at the drift of snow with one booted foot, gaze lowered so as not to meet his eyes. 'Have you?' he insisted softly, and she raised her eyes to meet the half-teasing, half-sympathetic gaze of his.

'I don't see that it concerns you,' she said, and heard him laugh.

'I rather thought it did,' he said. 'But if you say so——'

She looked across to where Richie was still intent on his fruitless task. 'I think it's time I took Richie home. I promised Mrs. Smith we wouldn't be very long.'

'Oh, you needn't bother about taking him home,' he told her airily. 'I can relieve you of the responsibility. As a matter of fact I called in on Effie Smith with the intention of collecting Richie and she told me you had taken him with you.' He smiled across at the boy. 'You like Richie, don't you?'

The question surprised her, but she managed to nod her head. 'Yes—yes, I do.'

The answer seemed to please him. 'I'm taking him into Cairndale for an hour or two.' He looked at her speculatively for a moment. 'Would you like to come too?' he asked.

'I—no, I don't think so, thank you.' She thought for a moment that he looked disappointed, but a second later the familiar mocking smile dispelled the impression.

'Afraid of Helen's tongue?' he taunted, and she flushed angrily at the near truth of the guess. She had no desire to antagonise Helen Murdoe further and if he was on such close terms with the other girl as she claimed, he should not have extended the invitation.

'I don't think you should have asked in the circumstances,' she retorted. 'Knowing how Miss Murdoe feels.'

He shrugged carelessly, his eyes dark with something that could have been anger glittering behind the laughter. 'I'm only concerned with how *I* feel,' he told her bluntly, and she shook her head over the sheer selfishness of the admission, though she doubted it to be true.

'I can believe it!' she retorted, and he laughed shortly, shaking his head.

'There you go again,' he told her. 'Oh, Paddy, you are a bundle of prickles, aren't you?'

'I'm no worse than anyone else,' she objected. 'And I thought you'd come to collect Richie, not to quarrel with me.'

'It's the other way round,' he told her, laughing, 'you quarrel with me.'

'I don't, I——' She bit her lip crossly. 'Take Richie and go,' she said, as if she had every right to order him off, and to her surprise he made no comment on it.

'You won't change your mind and come with us?'

'No—thank you.'

He eyed her steadily for a moment, then shrugged carelessly. 'O.K. If you don't want to come with us, fair enough. I'll take Richie and be gone.' He called the boy over and he came eagerly, his face shining with exertion, his smile anticipating a treat. 'Let's go,' Adam said briefly, and took his hand.

'Where to?' the boy asked. 'Where to, Adam?'

'Into Cairndale,' Adam told him, and looked again at Mora. Standing under the snow-covered branches of a fir tree, her dark hair straying from beneath the small woollen cap she wore, her cheeks softly pink from the sharp air, she had seldom looked lovelier than against that fairy-tale background and she was suddenly and disturbingly aware of it as he looked at her steadily.

'Mora too?' Richie asked, and Adam shook his head slowly.

'No,' he said quietly. 'Mora doesn't want to come with us.'

'Oh.' For a moment disappointment sobered the childish face, then the thought of the anticipated outing cheered him again. 'Let's go,' he urged. 'Come on, Adam.'

'Will you at least walk back as far as the cottage with

us?' Adam asked. 'I don't think Helen will object to that.' She made no reply, but left the sheltering tree and joined them on the narrow path, and the deep grey eyes gleamed with satisfaction, as at a victory.

CHAPTER SEVEN

It was a week later that Tizzy's son was born, and old Jeannie McKenzie was delighted to have another baby at Glen Ghyll, although Alison McLean had insisted on a younger professional nurse being brought in, and it had been left to Mora to comfort old Nana in her disappointment.

They drank champagne at dinner and the baby's health was toasted, his names ringing proudly round the walls of the old dining room. 'Duncan James Robert', names that had been in the McLean family for hundreds of years, but none of them Ian after his great-grandfather, Mora noticed a little sadly.

The new arrival was nearly a week old before Mora saw Adam again. She had just left her room and she saw him at the top of the stairs, looking unusually serious. His request that she accompany him to the north wing where old Ian McLean had had his rooms made her blink for a moment in surprise and uncertainty.

'Don't worry,' he told her wryly when she hesitated. 'I haven't any evil designs on you.'

The familiar resentment sparkled in her eyes as she looked at him. 'I didn't imagine you had,' she retorted, 'not with Hamish within calling distance!'

He laughed then and turned along the corridor to the north wing, presuming she would follow him—as she did. He strode ahead of her, his long legs making little of the distance; clad as usual in riding breeches and a thick sweater, arrogant and never doubting that she would do as he asked.

It felt strangely empty along the north wing now that the old man and Ramsey were no longer in occupation, and she found herself looking past the striding figure ahead of her to the dark blankness of the door into the tower room. The shade of the first Adam McLean seemed even closer now that the human tenants were no longer there, and she shuddered involuntarily.

Adam opened the door of what had been Ian McLean's sitting room and, entering, stood back to admit her before closing the door behind them and crossing to a big old-fashioned bureau against one wall.

The room still seemed to hold the spirit of the old man and at any moment Mora expected to hear his deep chuckle as she scored off Adam, or the weary sound of his voice when he was tired and refusing to give in to tiredness and pain. The feeling was so overwhelming that she stood near the door, her eyes fixed on the high winged chair the old man had always occupied, tears misting her vision when she saw it empty.

'Would you rather not have come, Mora?' Adam's voice was more like his grandfather's than she had ever realised before and she shook her head, brushing a hand across the tears.

'It's—it's all right,' she said, her voice husky. 'It was just that, for a moment——'

'He still seems to be here, doesn't he?' he asked softly, and came across to her, standing so that his body blocked her view of the empty chair. 'I'm sorry. Perhaps I shouldn't have brought you here. I forget that you were so fond of the old man. You knew him such a little time, but you seemed to mean a great deal to each other in those few weeks.'

'I *was* very fond of him,' she admitted, aware of the gentleness in his eyes as he watched her. 'I—I think perhaps it was because I never knew my own grandfather, he seemed to take his place in a way. But I don't mind coming here; please don't apologise.' It was, she thought ironically, the most amiable conversation they had ever had in this room, and she wondered if the old man would have been disappointed in them.

'There was something he wanted you to have,' he told her, turning back to the bureau. 'I thought you'd like it now, before all his things are moved.' He lifted the top of the desk and took out a fairly large oblong package wrapped in hessian. 'I took it down from his bedroom as he asked me to,' he explained. 'I'm one of his executors, so it's quite all right for me to give it to you.'

'Thank you.' She took the package from him, her eyes uncertain as she looked at it. 'May I—may I look at it now?' she asked, and he nodded. She put it down on the small table she had so often used as a writing desk when the old man was talking, and unfolded the hessian cautiously, her heart hammering against her ribs, though she could not imagine why she should feel so tensely expectant.

The face that looked up at her from the painting could have been her own. Only the hair was lighter brown and piled on top of the head in an elaborate coiffure, and the eyes were perhaps less blue than grey and the chin and mouth less wilful in expression—demurely sweet in the fashion of her day, but the shape and structure of the face and the way the head was held were almost exact replicas of her own.

'She's lovely, isn't she?' Adam asked quietly from just behind her.

Mora nodded agreement, unable to deny the truth of it, however much the woman resembled herself. 'Who is she?' she asked.

He laughed softly. 'Don't you recognise your own image?' She raised puzzled eyes to him and he smiled teasingly. 'Her name,' he told her, 'was Marie Forbes.'

'My grandmother!' She looked again at the serene and lovely face in the painting and tilted her head to one side to study it. '*Am* I like her, Adam?'

'You are,' he assured her, and added, 'And that's the first time you've called me Adam. I hope you won't stop there.'

She hastily looked back at the painting. 'She's the one who eloped with Robert McLean, isn't she?'

'She is,' he agreed. 'As Grandfather told you more than once, the McLeans have a habit of stealing each other's women.'

'But not necessarily murdering their husbands to do it!' she replied, remembering his namesake's contribution to the legend, and also his own.

Adam laughed. 'Some women are worth it,' he said softly, an observation she chose to ignore.

'I'm glad I'm able to have this picture,' she told him. 'I'm grateful to Grandfather McLean for thinking of me. I've never seen my grandmother at all. I *have* seen a couple of old photographs of my grandfather, but Marie, his wife, died about the end of the first war, I believe, and there was nothing of her at all.' She frowned suddenly as the thought struck her. 'How is it that this branch of the family had this painting and not my grandfather?' she asked.

'Simple,' he replied with a smile. 'But for Robert McLean's bit of skulduggery in eloping with her, she would have been my *great*-grandmother and hanging among the portraits on the staircase wall. It seems old Duncan McLean couldn't bring himself to part with the painting of his lost love and he kept it. Ten years ago, when he died, my grandfather inherited it and he too found the fair Marie irresistible.' The deep eyes studied her seriously for a moment. 'He was quite bowled over when you arrived here with Hamish, you know. It was as if his favourite painting had come to life. That's why he wanted you to——' He stopped short, serious still for a moment, then the famliar laugh mocked both her and himself. 'Anyway, you now have a grandmama, and no one can deny *that* ancestry, can they?'

'I don't think so,' she said quietly, though her heart was behaving so erratically that she felt sure he must hear it. She covered the painted face again with the protective hessian and picked it up from the table. 'I shall hang it in my sitting room and look at her often.'

He narrowed his eyes for a moment. 'In London?' he asked, and she nodded. 'So you are going back—I wondered if—— When are you thinking of going?'

'I—I don't know,' she said, wondering why it seemed so important to him to know and if Helen Murdoe had asked him to find out. 'Soon. I must, I've been here so long now and the longer I stay the harder it becomes to think of leaving.'

'Then why leave?' he asked, as if it was the most reasonable question in the world. 'You rent a room here, don't you?' She nodded, surprised at his knowledge and, sensing her surprise, he smiled. 'I suppose it was put on a business footing so that Hamish would know where he stands, is that it?'

'I—I don't really see that it concerns you,' she said, unwilling to face the fact that their truce seemed to be at an end and that she regretted it more than she cared to admit.

'Perhaps not,' he admitted blandly, 'but I'd like to know just the same. *Are* you going to marry Hamish?'

'I've told you,' she said. 'It——'

'It's none of my business—I know.' He took the picture from her and moved towards the door. 'I'll carry this for you.' She followed him to the door, turning to take a last look at the familiar room and the empty chair by the window. It would be hard to leave Glen Ghyll, even now that old Ian was gone, but she supposed it would soon be inevitable, and she sighed as she turned away, her eyes wistful.

'Don't sigh for him, Mora,' Adam said softly from close beside her as he leaned across to close the door. 'He was in dreadful pain and he went peacefully.' He hesitated, seeming to be uncertain about something he wanted to say. 'There was something else——' he began, then shook his head. 'No, never mind now—it can wait.'

In the corridor once more, her eyes were drawn again to the dark door at the end of it and, following her gaze,

Adam smiled. 'You never did see the north tower or old Adam's ghost, did you?'

'No,' she said. 'I'd like to before I go.'

'Which?' he asked, laughing. 'The tower room or the old villain's ghost?' It was a challenge and she knew it, feeling her blood rise to it.

'Both!' she retorted, and his deep laugh echoed the length of the corridor.

'It's a challenge,' he told her, his eyes glittering in the last of the daylight from the long windows. 'You come back here after dinner, when it's really dark, and see if the old reprobate will appear for you.' He looked like his namesake as he stood there, daring her to refuse, much as the original Adam might have challenged his secret lover to a rendez-vous under the very nose of her husband. And, as Marjorie Stewart McLean had done, she accepted the dare because she was unable to resist it.

'Alone?' she asked.

He smiled. 'That's up to you. You can ask Hamish to hold your hand if you want to, or—me. He's more likely to appear for me; we're kindred spirits, you see, he wouldn't like Hamish at all.'

For a moment she looked at him, almost holding her breath to resist the temptation he offered, knowing that he was fully aware of her feelings and revelling in them. 'I'll ask Hamish to come with me,' she told him at last, and saw disappointment cloud his eyes briefly before the familiar laughter returned.

'Suit yourself,' he said, 'but don't say I didn't warn you. Old Adam may not appear for Hamish, unless it's to frighten the wits out of him for the sheer fun of it.'

'You must be even more alike than I thought,' she re-torted. 'That's the kind of thing you'd do.'

'Is it?' He looked surprised for a moment. 'You *have* got a poor opinion of me, haven't you, Paddy? I wonder what would redeem me in your eyes.' He studied her specula-tively for a moment in the fading daylight. 'Or perhaps nothing would,' he added resignedly, and laughed softly. 'You marry brother Hamish, Mora, and then at least we'll have the pleasure of seeing you in the portrait gallery, or our descendants will. Robert McLean deprived us of the lovely Marie, perhaps Hamish can remedy that by bringing us her granddaughter.'

'I—I don't think I shall ever be marrying Hamish,' she said, without quite knowing why she was being so frank with him. 'I don't know how I feel. I know your grandfather wanted me to marry him, but I couldn't promise that, not even for him.'

'He wanted you——' He frowned for a moment, then she saw the white gleam of his smile. 'Oh yes, the old man asked you to marry his grandson. I remember now—I'd forgotten he'd done that.'

Mora studied his face, trying to judge his expression. 'But how do you know that?' she asked. 'You weren't there, you were waiting for the doctor.'

'Ramsey was there,' he said simply. and her question was answered.

Hamish thought her request to visit the north tower a silly one and he said so when she asked him to accompany her. 'What's the point?' he asked. 'You don't really believe in ghosts, do you?'

'Of course I don't,' she laughed, 'but I would like to see the other tower room, and besides——' She hesitated to mention Adam's challenge for fear he thought her even more silly for accepting it.

'Besides?' he prompted.

'I *must* go now,' she said, flushing at the look he gave her. 'Adam dared me to.'

He stared at her for a moment in disbelief and she thought how differently his brother would have reacted to such a challenge. 'Adam? What does he think he's up to? The tower rooms are never used now, they haven't been for centuries—well, for over a hundred years anyway.' Something about her words made him frown suddenly and he

105

looked down at her with drawn brows. 'You said the *other* tower room; you've never been in either of them, have you?'

She realised that having said so much she must tell him the rest, although she hated to think what his reaction would be. At least, she decided, there was no need to mention the intimacy of the last occasion. 'I've been to the south tower,' she said. 'In fact I've been twice, actually.'

'When?' He sounded as angry as she had expected him to, and she wished she had never mentioned the silly ghost, transferring the blame for her position, as usual, to Adam.

'The first time was just after I arrived,' she said. 'And the second time was the night before your grandfather died.'

'And both times with Adam, I suppose?' She found it hard to bear the faint sneer in his voice and felt her colour rise warmly in her cheeks.

'Yes,' she admitted. 'I saw no harm in going with your brother, Hamish. It was cold, but very refreshing up there in the wind.'

'I'm sure it was,' he said sarcastically. 'I suppose you realise that's where his namesake used to take his brother's wife for their secret meetings? It seems history *does* repeat itself.'

His condemnation angered her until she clenched her hands into fists at her sides and her eyes sparkled with it. 'With two big differences,' she said tartly. 'I'm *not* your wife and Adam is *not* my lover—and if you want to make a mountain out of a molehill, go ahead, but get the facts right first!'

He was silent for a moment, watching her angry face, her dark-fringed eyes blazing at him. 'I'm sorry, darling,' he said at last, and using an endearment he seldom used. 'But you know why I was so mad about you being with Adam, you know quite well. I'm sorry.'

'Oh, it doesn't matter, Hamish.' She dismissed it lightly, though his sarcasm still rankled in her mind and the implications he had made about her being with Adam. She looked at him enquiringly, her head tilted to one side. 'Are you coming with me to the north tower, or shall I go alone?'

'Would you dare?' he asked. For a moment he looked very like Adam and she felt something of the same excitement stir in her that his brother always aroused.

'Of course I would,' she declared, and hoped she would not be called upon to prove it. Hamish laughed and put an arm round her shoulders, hugging her close for a second.

'Come along then, my intrepid ghost-hunter, let's go and see if old Adam will appear for us.'

'Your brother doesn't think he will,' she ventured as they left the big room and crossed the hall to the stairs.

He pulled a wry face. 'Well, for once I can't help but agree with him.' Mora laughed a little dizzily as they mounted a wide staircase under the painted gaze of the man whose ghost they sought. 'Mind you,' Hamish murmured darkly as they passed the portrait, 'I wouldn't put it past him to have arranged something up there. They're too much alike for comfort, those two.'

She remembered her own remarks in that direction, but refrained from repeating them. She remembered too the way history had repeated itself with regard to Helen Murdoe and Hamish himself and wondered if now was a good time to bring up the subject.

'They are alike,' she agreed. 'And in more ways than one.' Sensing something in her words more than she actually said, he looked down at her, mildly curious, his arm still about her shoulders as they climbed the stairs. 'Hamish, was it—was it Adam who caused the break between—between you and Helen Murdoe?'

She saw the dark flush of anger mount his face from neck to hairline and he scowled blackly, his arm stiffening on her shoulders. 'I suppose Adam told you that,' he said coldly. 'You two are on even more confiding terms than I feared.' He drew a deep breath, as if it helped to control some emotion almost too strong for him. 'Yes, he was the reason Helen broke our engagement and then he behaved in the only way a man like that *could* behave. He refused to marry her and instead cleared off into the blue for nearly six years.'

'Is that why——?' She could not bring herself to ask the question outright, but he followed her train of thought and laughed harshly.

'That's partly why he's not popular with the rest of us,' he said. 'He left Helen in the most embarrassing position and just went off. Left her alone to face the humiliation of being jilted by her lover.'

'Like she jilted you?' Mora suggested softly, and felt him start in surprise, his eyes turned on her searchingly.

'Are you defending him?' he asked, and she met his gaze defiantly, her cheeks softly flushed as she admitted it.

'I just believe that what is sauce for the goose is sauce for the gander,' she said, and he was silent for a moment while they turned into the long carpeted length of the north wing.

'It's not the same thing,' he said at last. 'Helen was quite honest about her feelings and she broke off the engagement in the proper manner. We've known the Murdoes all our lives, and Adam's behaviour was unforgivable.'

'Except to Helen,' Mora said, and again sensed his surprise.

'There's nothing between them now as far as I know,' he said. 'Helen recovered from whatever it was she felt for Adam, a long time ago.'

'Not according to Helen,' Mora insisted. 'That's why she——' She bit her lip, knowing that to mention Helen Murdoe's suspicions with regard to herself and Adam would only add to what Hamish himself now suspected.

'Why she what?' he asked, and she shook her head, laughing as they approached the heavy wooden door into the tower room.

'Nothing. Now shush—ghosts don't appear if you talk too loudly.'

He turned the heavy ring handle and the door creaked open, letting out that damp, cold smell of neglect that its twin had. The room looked exactly the same except that the long leg of the L was to the right instead of left and one or two items of furniture stood shadowy dark in the faint moonlight, filtering in through the slit windows.

Hamish led the way, crossing to the nearest window and sniffing the cold air from outside, deeply. 'It smells like a tomb in here,' he said disgustedly, and Mora could not restrain a rather nervous laugh.

'Old Adam died in here, didn't he?' she asked, joining him beside the glassless strip of window.

'He did. Of old age and good living,' he sounded bitterly rueful. 'They say the devil looks after his own, and there never was a truer case than Adam McLean.'

'Aren't you being a little unfair?' Mora objected, amused by his opinion of his ancestor in contrast to his brother's. 'Things were very much different then and morals rather more lax than now—perhaps. Apart from that one lapse, he might not have been a *bad* man.'

He turned a gaze on her that could have belonged to a latter-day John Knox. 'Adultery? Murder? Treason? How many lapses is a man allowed before *you* condemn him, Mora?' He sounded so deadly serious and Mora wished she had not asked him to come with her, since he seemed unable to forgive even after two and a half centuries. He would be a hard man, she thought, and quite unrelenting no matter who was concerned, and for some reason the realisation made her shiver far more than the prospect of Adam McLean's ghost.

'I think circumstances have a lot to do with it,' she said. 'And don't forget that it takes two to make a bargain like Marjorie and Adam made. She was as black as he was, it's not fair that Adam should carry all the blame.' She spoke of his ancestors, but her thoughts included his brother and Helen Murdoe in the plea and, from his answer, he might have guessed it.

'A man with his heart set on seduction usually succeeds,' he said shortly. 'There's no excuse, Mora, none at all.'

'Then I just have to disagree,' Mora said softly. 'No woman can be seduced unless she's ready and willing to be.' She studied his face in the almost dark; the glittering eyes and dark head could have belonged to Adam, only the mockery and the tense excitement were missing, and she shook herself hastily to dispel the image of his brother. 'Let's go back to civilisation,' she said lightly. 'Your wicked ancestor isn't going to appear tonight.'

'I never expected he would,' he said, making an effort to relieve the atmosphere that seemed to have settled around them in the dank coldness of the room. 'It's not one of his nights for visiting, obviously.'

'Obviously,' Mora echoed as she followed him to the door. She turned as she left the big, cold room and smiled briefly at the shadows of the furniture in the long slivers of moonlight.

Adam had been right—his namesake would never appear for such a disappointing descendant as Hamish, and it must have been her imagination, or the wind through the open slit windows that made her hear a soft sigh of laughter just before Hamish closed the door with a resounding thud.

CHAPTER EIGHT

IT was Christmas Eve when Mora finally got up enough will power to decide to leave Glen Ghyll. She had done all that she could do to her book on the family McLean and there was absolutely no reason for her to stay on at the castle any longer. After two months she would find it a wrench to leave, but there were limits to even Highland hospitality and she was paying far less for her room at Glen Ghyll than she should have been.

When she announced her intention at dinner, however, Sir James fixed her with his fierce blue eyes and frowned his displeasure at the news. 'I don't see why you have to go, my dear,' he told her, with a reasoning reminiscent of both Adam and Hamish. 'We like having you here. Pretty girl about the old place, hmm?' He looked across at Hamish, his expression half amused, half impatient. 'I should have thought Hamish could have talked you round to his way of thinking by now,' he went on, and Mora flushed at the frankness that was so typical of him.

'Hamish and I are good friends, Sir James, nothing more.'

'Then it's time you were,' Sir James retorted. 'I'd married and fathered three sons before I was Hamish's age.'

Mora saw the dark flush that coloured Hamish's face and felt sorry for him as the brunt of his father's unfortunate lack of tact. 'There's really no urgent necessity for me to marry, Father,' he said quietly. 'And I'm sure Mora and I can manage our own affairs without the benefit of your advice.'

'Maybe, maybe,' Sir James allowed grudgingly. 'But

can't you talk Mora into staying a while longer at least? Damn it,' he added explosively, 'I'm fond of the gel. I've a mind to marry her myself if she'll have me. Will you, Mora?'

'James, stop embarrassing the poor girl,' Alison McLean admonished, and leaned across the table to touch Mora's hand in sympathy. 'Take no notice of him, my dear, it's a failing in this family. The men can never resist pretty girls or trying to take someone else's.' It was an unusually gentle and understanding gesture from the normally brusque woman, and Mora smiled her gratitude. Hamish, seated next to his aunt, looked as black as thunder.

'It's very sweet of everyone to be so kind,' Mora told them. 'I love it at Glen Ghyll, but I *have* been here a long time and I feel you must want to return to being just family, without a—a lodger always under your feet and sharing your table.'

'Nonsense, child!' Alison McLean said brusquely. 'You *are* family. Your McLean blood may be two generations away, but you're still family, and as such you're welcome here for as long as you can put up with us.'

Mora laughed. 'I rather thought it was the other way round,' she said. 'You were putting up with me.' She shook her head uncertainly. 'The temptation to stay on is enormous,' she admitted, 'but what possible reason have I for staying? I've done all I can do to my book, so the research reason is no longer valid.'

'You don't need a reason, do you?' Sir James asked. 'And if you do, then what about acting as secretary to me? I have a heck of a lot of work to do at home here, and someone to take down notes and type would make things very much easier for me.'

Mora hesitated, suspecting that the offer of employment was just as an excuse to keep her there. Sir James was quite fond of her, she realised, but not in the way he had implied with his facetious offer of marriage. Hamish had confided too her earlier that his father had always wanted a daughter, and perhaps Mora, with her McLean blood and a certain family likeness, seemed to him the nearest he would ever come to achieving his wish. She smiled at him, her wide blue eyes soft with understanding. 'Thank you, Sir James, if you really mean that, I'd like to work for you.'

'I *do* mean it, my dear.' The broad face beamed delightedly at her. 'You'll stay?'

'Thank you, I'd like to.'

'Good, good.' He nodded his satisfaction and looked across at Hamish. 'There you are, you see, it just takes a little ingenuity.' Hamish, Mora felt, could have looked more pleased, but she suspected that his father's lack of tact was the reason for his frown rather than the fact that she was to stay on.

Alison McLean smiled her approval and only Fergus looked doubtful, but made no comment as he stirred sugar into his coffee. Mora could not help but wonder what Adam's reaction to the arrangement would be.

Christmas Day dawned crisp and cold and with a new layer of snow to cover the muddy remains of the old and give the countryside a Christmas-card look that Mora found enchanting, especially when the wintry sun shone palely from the grey blue sky.

It saddened her to notice that not even the season of good will could induce the family to invite Adam to join them, and she thought of him in the little keeper's cottage just a few hundred yards away. Whether he would be alone or not she had no way of knowing. Perhaps he would be spending some of the time with Helen Murdoe and her mother in the big, gloomy stone house at the edge of Glencairn, and somehow that prospect pleased her even less.

The thought of what Helen Murdoe's reaction would be to her own continued stay at Glen Ghyll did not bear thinking about, so she dismissed it for the time being.

She sat with Hamish in the window of the big room after lunch, far enough away from the rest of the family to be able to talk freely without being heard, and the subject uppermost in her mind came easily to her tongue as they looked out at the sun glinting on fresh snow. 'I wondered if Adam might be here,' she ventured, 'as it's Christmas.'

Hamish turned curious eyes to her, a slight frown between his brows as if the exclusion of his brother from the family circle worried him to a certain extent too. 'It's the way he wants it,' he told her, unconsciously echoing Adam.

'Is it, Hamish?' Her deep blue eyes with their thick fringe of lashes might have been pleading as they looked at him, and he turned away, shaking his head uncertainly.

'I don't know,' he admitted, 'but it's the way things are and it's not my place to change them.'

'Or mine either, is that what you mean?' she asked, and her smile took the sting from the words.

Hamish shook his head. 'I wasn't hinting, Mora. It's—it's just that we know all the facts and you don't. There's more than you realise behind Adam's reputation as a—a——'

'A black sheep?' Mora suggested gently. 'Yes, I gathered there was, Hamish, but it isn't my place to ask questions. I'm not trying to pry, please don't think that.'

'I didn't,' he assured her hastily, and frowned his uncertainty, as if he doubted the wisdom of what he wanted to say. 'It's—it's the boy, you see.'

Mora looked puzzled. 'The boy? Richie, you mean?' Hamish nodded, still without looking at her, a certain tenseness in him that she suspected was reluctance to discuss his brother. 'What has the boy to do with it? Only if you want to tell me, of course,' she added hastily.

He sat silently unanswering for a moment or two, then turned his head and looked at her, his eyes anxious, as if he feared her reaction. 'Don't you know about him?' he asked. 'I thought perhaps you would, being friendly with Adam.' There was bitterness in the last words, and she wondered resignedly if he ever forgave anyone anything.

'I've seen the boy several times,' she admitted. 'He's a

114

nice child and I know Effie Smith only takes care of him, but that's the extent of my knowledge. His name's Richie Gordon. I know that too.' He said nothing, but continued to look at her, willing her to understand something that Mora's heart refused to believe but which her head already admitted as truth.

'He's his son,' Hamish said at last, with the same bitterness he had used to condemn the first Adam McLean in the tower room only two days ago.

Mora shook her head. The pulse in her temple throbbed dizzily as it did whenever Adam was gentle or teasing with her, only this time it was despair that set her blood racing through her head. Anger and despair. 'Adam's son?'

Hamish nodded, sensing less of her emotions than she feared.

'You see why he's not wanted here,' he said, as if she could only agree with the decision. 'First there was the business of Helen, and then, when he finally came back here, he brought that boy with him from Australia.'

Mora did not comment, instead staring out at the sun-sparkled snow on the graceful nakedness of the trees, seeing the grey eyes of Richie Gordon and the dark hair and the curiously familiar gestures he used. Remembering, too, the rapport between him and Adam that she had noticed from the beginning and his evasion of any question concerning Richie's name.

'He's very like him,' she said, trying not to sound as flatly empty as she felt suddenly.

'Unfortunately for him!' Hamish retorted, stung perhaps by her apparent acceptance of the fact. 'He can scarcely deny his existence.'

'Has he tried to?' she asked quietly, and sensed his resentment of the question.

'No,' he admitted.

'It would have been simple, I would have thought,' Mora pointed out, 'to have left the boy in Australia and none of you need ever have known of his existence.' She looked at

115

him squarely, the light of challenge in her blue eyes, surprising even herself with her defence of Adam McLean. 'It's what most men would have done,' she said, and defied him to argue.

Hamish's dark brows drew together in a frown. 'Are you defending him?' he asked, and Mora shook her head, looking down at her fingers in her lap, realising how it must have sounded to him.

'I don't think I need to,' she said, half to herself. 'Adam can take care of himself.'

He watched her silently for a moment or two, then took her hands between his own, a smile on his face as he sought to dispel the chill between them. 'It's Christmas Day,' he said lightly. 'We should be bright and cheerful.' He leaned across and kissed her gently beside her mouth. 'I still want to marry you,' he said softly, 'any time you'll have me, Mora.'

If Mora was more quiet than usual for the rest of the day no one appeared to notice, except perhaps Hamish, and she went to her room that night feeling more unhappy than she had since old Ian McLean's death. She closed the door of her room on Hamish's whispered 'Goodnight' and sank gratefully on to the soft mound of the old feather bed, feeling unutterably weary and very close to tears, though she scolded herself for a fool for being so emotional about a man who was, self-admittedly, no better than he should be.

The next day was clear and frost-sparkling with the sun already making snow and ice drip like diamonds from trees and eaves and promising another fine day. It would be clear enough on the road for her to walk as far as Glencairn and the exercise would perhaps help to dispel some of the oppression she felt still.

Hamish offered to accompany her, but she pleaded a headache and the need for solitude as a cure. The snow was clearing much faster than she had realised, though there

116

were still quite deep drifts of it on corners and against the bushes that grew along the road. It was quite easy walking on the narrow little road, although it was slushy, and she was glad of her high boots for protection.

She enjoyed the crisp coldness of the air and felt her cheeks colour rosily in the sharp wind as she walked. Glencairn seemed nearer than usual, thanks to her preoccupation, and she found herself passing Helen Murdoe's house almost before she realised it.

The tall trees hid most of the windows from the road, but one looked out over a square of snow-covered lawn and as she passed Mora saw a faint flutter of movement at the old-fashioned lace curtains. A moment later the front door of the house opened and Helen Murdoe appeared.

'Good morning.' The soft voice was raised in greeting and Mora's intuition warned her that the apparent friendliness of the girl hid an ulterior motive. However, she raised a hand in greeting and Helen came down to the gate. 'You'll be on one of your long walks?' she said, her beautiful eyes studying Mora's rose-tinged cheeks and bright eyes.

'I had a headache,' Mora said, warily agreeable. Evidently the seasonal spirit had touched the other girl, or so it would appear. 'I find a walk is the best cure.'

'I thought you'd maybe have gone home for Christmas,' said Helen Murdoe. 'Christmas to the English is a big family affair, is it not?'

'It is,' Mora admitted, 'but my parents are abroad and I'm an only child. There's no one else to bother with, and I *am* with my own people in a way.' She could not resist the reminder, though she was possibly being uncharitable, she thought.

The oddly attractive face smiled wryly. 'Oh yes, of course, you're Robert McLean's granddaughter, aren't you? I would hardly have thought that anyone from that branch of the family, however remote, was welcome at Glen Ghyll.'

Mora smiled tightly, a sparkle of anger in her blue eyes.

'I don't think Sir James and his family are likely to be small-minded enough to let ancient history influence them,' she said, forgetting for the moment that Adam was suffering from just such a prejudice. 'In fact Sir James has been kind enough to ask me to work for him after Christmas, so I shall be staying for some time yet.'

The silence that greeted the news was ominous, and Mora wondered if she had been unduly rash in mentioning what was, after all, only a tentative arrangement as yet. 'Congratulations.' The soft voice had an edge as chill as ice and the dark eyes glowed angrily, though Helen did her best to appear normally polite. 'I've no doubt Hamish will be very pleased about it.'

Mora merely nodded, making no comment on Hamish's feelings in the matter. 'Ah well,' Helen Murdoe said, looking along the road to where the two ways forked, one the way Mora had come from Glen Ghyll and the other the way that ran round the loch, 'I'll go into the warm again and let you get on. The snow's clearing well; I noticed this morning that even the way round the loch is clear.'

Mora blinked her doubt at the information, although the portion of track that she could see looked clear enough. 'You've been riding this morning?'

'Oh yes.' Her laugh was as soft as her voice and managed to convey the same chilling quality. 'I was brought up round here, you know, I've never been afraid of it.' The implication was unmistakable, and Mora flushed at it while the dark eyes added their weight to the challenge. 'It's even fit to walk round that way, if you're not afraid of getting lost, of course.'

Mora's hesitation was only brief. 'If you think it's fit to walk that way,' she said, 'I think I'll go back by way of the loch.' For a moment the glitter in the girl's eyes troubled her, but she told herself that if it was too bad, she could always turn round and come back, rejoining the road she had come along.

She waved a casual hand as she started off and she was

aware of Helen Murdoe watching her from the gate even as she turned on to the path beside the loch, a look on her face that made Mora uneasy.

The path was, as the other girl had said, quite clear enough for walking and the loch had a special kind of beauty after snow. A lacy edge of it frilled the stones and hung from the stunted trees and bushes that bordered it, slowly vanishing as the pale sun grew stronger, dropping soundlessly into the almost black water.

There were tall sweeps of it here and there where the wind had blown it into deep drifts and an occasional hard hump of it meant climbing over them for she would not risk going into the softer and possibly deeper snow alongside. At times she found herself almost calf deep over these humps of snow, thanking heaven for her boots. It was hard going at times, but Mora felt it was worth the effort, for the scene it presented was enchanting.

Looking ahead and to her right she could just see the little stone hut where she and Adam had sheltered from the storm. It was strange, she thought, that she had ridden this way with Hamish several times and never noticed the little building, perhaps because it was so small and blended so well into its background.

Glancing up, she thought she saw a puff of white smoke from the short square chimney, but it was most likely snow, blown into powdery swirls by the wind. She would never see that little hut again without being reminded of that storm, or of Adam.

Thinking of Adam, she frowned. It should not have been such a shock to her to learn that Richie Gordon was Adam's son, but somehow it had been—not because of the moral laxity involved, but because he did not boast of it. Adam would, she thought, have been daredevil enough to be proud of the boy and let everyone know who he was. It would have been more in keeping with the image of the original Adam. That he had kept it a secret *had* been a shock to her.

She was preoccupied completely with her thoughts and the thought of how he had evaded the question of Richie's name and how he had laughed at her so often angered her afresh. What a fool he must have thought her for not seeing the truth!

Another mound of snow, somewhat higher than the others, blocked her path and she prepared to climb over it as she had done before, leaning her weight forward to give her a foothold on the packed snow. Too late she realised that this was not a low drift like the others she had climbed over but one which hid a deep depression in the ground.

She had been so preoccupied with her thoughts of Adam McLean that she had completely forgotten the deep dip in the path that they had skirted round when she had been riding with Hamish, and she opened her mouth in an involuntary scream of realisation as the soft snow gave under her and she fell deeper and deeper into it.

Surprisingly, after the first chilling plunge, it felt almost warm and indescribably soft as she struggled to find a firm footing to help her and found none. The more she struggled the deeper she went, and there seemed to be no bottom to the depression.

Her breath soon became erratic and laboured as the snow engulfed her and she found it difficult to keep her head clear of it, until finally common sense told her that, going on as she was, she was only making her position worse and she stopped struggling.

As she lay there, half buried, great tears of sheer panic rolled down her cheeks and her heart threatened to burst from her body with the speed and heaviness of its pounding. She recognised with horrible certainty that Helen Murdoe had foreseen this happening and had deliberately suggested that she walk back this way, making the suggestion a challenge that she knew Mora would be unable to resist.

Suddenly she opened her eyes, realising with horror that the soft snow had induced a state of lethargy in her that was hard to resist. She shook her head, trying to see along the path she had come, but it was a vain hope, she realised, to think that anyone else would be foolish enough to venture along this path on foot. She must help herself, if she could.

She tried again for some sort of foothold, but there seemed to be none, and she felt the tears roll down her cheeks dismally while she raised her voice as best she could for her position and called for help, all the time fighting to stave off that dangerous lethargy that wanted her to give in and just sink blissfully down into the soft whiteness.

How long she called or how long it was before she finally surrendered to the heaviness of her limbs and eyelids, she had no idea, but she was aware, slowly, of warmth and hardness under her and of a voice that sounded a long way off.

'Mora! Mora!' She tried to open her eyes, but the lids still felt unbelievably heavy and refused to open. 'Mora!' A sharp slap on one cheek jerked her drowsy mind into some sort of activity and she turned her head protestingly. 'Mora!' Another slap stung the other cheek and at last she managed to raise her eyelids to glare at her attacker. 'Wake up, come on!'

'Go 'way,' she mumbled crossly, closing her eyes again. She felt herself raised slightly by a strong arm that held her half upright, shaking her determinedly to wake her up.

'Not until you wake up,' Adam told her. 'Come *on*, Mora. Wake up!'

She managed to make her eyes stay open at last and blinked at him slowly, a frown between her brows when she saw the look of anxiety on his face. 'Adam?'

'Who else?' he retorted, pulling her upright into a sitting position, and still keeping an arm round her shoulders. 'Drink this.' He thrust a thick mug of steaming black coffee against her lips and she shuddered.

'Ugh!' she protested. 'It's black!'

'Drink it,' he ordered, 'or I'll hold your nose and pour it down the way they do with children.' She thought from the

121

glitter in his eyes that he meant it, so she sipped cautiously at the thick black brew and pulled a face. 'Don't fuss,' he added. 'It's hot and strong, and that's what you need. Drink!'

She obediently swallowed another mouthful or two, then shook her head. 'No more, please.' She was, she noticed, covered with his jacket and her own soaking wet coat lay in a crumpled heap on the floor near the hearth.

She sat right in front of a blazing fire that made her fingers and toes tingle with the warmth of returning circulation until they hurt painfully. He put down the mug on the hearth and turned back to look at her.

'How do you feel?'

'Better—I think.' She struggled to sit more upright and without his support and he helped her, kneeling on the hard floor beside her. He took her hands between his, rubbing her fingers into life, while she bit her lip on the pain of reviving circulation. 'Do they really do that?' she asked suddenly, and he glanced up at her with a raised and curious brow.

'What are you talking about now?'

'Do they really give children things by holding their noses and pouring it down?'

He grinned at her, concentrating again on his task. 'I wouldn't know,' he said. 'I seem to remember something in Dickens—anyway it seemed like a good idea.'

'I don't think so,' she said, finding her lips curiously stiff and cold as she spoke, despite the hot coffee.

'How in heaven's name did you manage to be out there in that predicament?' he asked, and she did not immediately answer. In her mind was the all too clear picture of Helen Murdoe telling her that the path round the loch was clear enough for walking, but how much of the truth would Adam read into the incident if she told him?

'I thought that path was clear,' she said, through her stiff lips. 'My face feels stiff,' she added complainingly, and would have put her hands to it, but he still held them.

'You're lucky not to be stiff all over!' he retorted. 'Permanently!' Seeing her bite her lip painfully in an effort to stem the tears of reaction that filled her eyes, he dropped her hands and put his own either side of her face, the warmth of them making her cheeks tingle. 'I'm sorry, Mora, I shouldn't yell at you. You're cold and frightened and all I do is scold you. I'm sorry.' The deep grey eyes were gentle as they looked down at her and she felt the familiar throb of the pulse in her temple.

'It *was* my own fault really,' she admitted, wishing he would not look at her so intently or rub her cold cheeks in that soothing, gentle way that made her feel sleepy.

'Why did you come that way?' he asked. 'You left by the Glencairn road, didn't you?'

'Yes—and I would have come back that way too, but——'

'But?' he prompted, and she tried to turn her head away, but he held her firm, his eyes searching her face. 'What or who changed your mind, Mora?'

'Helen Murdoe,' she admitted reluctantly, and frowned her annoyance when he laughed.

'Go on,' he encouraged, still smiling.

'It's not funny,' she protested. 'I don't expect you to believe me when she's your—when you're such close friends.'

'Never mind how close friends I am with Helen,' he told her. 'Tell me how you came to be along the loch path when it was obviously so much safer to go back the way you came, along the road.'

She hesitated, while he still held her facing him, his hands again soothing and warming her tingling face. 'She said she'd ridden along the path this morning and it was clear enough for walking. It wasn't too bad,' she added in fairness, 'but I forgot that deep hollow in the ground just there and I was—I was thinking of something else. Before I knew where I was, I'd fallen into that drift and I couldn't get out again.' Telling him rekindled some of the panic she had felt and she shivered, her eyes wide and frightened. 'I

123

was so afraid. I just couldn't free myself and I thought——'
Tears rolled down her face again and she felt miserably
forlorn, curled up on the floor in front of the fire, her hair
clinging wetly to her head.

'Well, you didn't,' he said softly, 'so stop crying over it.'
He looked down at her for a second in silence, then he put
his arms round her tightly, holding her close, his face resting on the soft dampness of her hair. 'You always seem to
look like a wet puppy when I rescue you,' he teased her. 'I
didn't stop to rescue your hat either, I was too busy getting
you out.'

She made a muffled protest at the 'wet puppy', but was
content, for the moment, to stay where she was. Only the
faint click of hooves on stone made her raise her head after
a moment, a frown of query between her brows as she
looked at Adam. 'Who is it?' she asked, hearing the telltale
flinty click again.

He got to his feet and went to the small window to look
out, and a moment later she heard him laugh softly as he
turned to her. 'Brother Hamish,' he said, his smile half
puzzled, half derisive. 'Now why, I wonder, is *he* out
here?'

'You were,' she pointed out reasonably, and he laughed
again.

'I was,' he admitted. 'And fortunately Klonda caught a
stone and hurt a leg or I wouldn't have been here when you
dived into that snowdrift.'

'Oh, is *that* how you came to rescue me?'

'Sheer luck,' he said. 'I had to rest Klonda before I took
him home and I'd made a fire and some coffee, so everything was laid on for you.'

'I'm grateful,' she said, and he raised his eyebrows, half
mocking her.

'Are you?'

She could hear the jingle of the harness outside and the
sound of footsteps near the door of the hut.

'Adam?' Hamish's voice sounded unusually loud as he

opened the door and put his head inside. The first person he saw was Mora, curled up like a kitten before the fire, with Adam's coat over her legs, her face flushed rosily from the fire and Adam's gentle administrations. 'Mora!'

'Hello, Hamish.' She could find no other words and knew from the darkness of his eyes that he read the worst into her being there.

He turned his gaze to his brother, standing by the window. 'I was going to ask you if you'd seen Mora,' he said stiffly, 'but I see I have no need to worry about her any further. I'm sorry I intruded.'

'Hamish——!'

'For heaven's sake don't be such a fool,' Adam told him brusquely. 'Hear what happened first before you go off half cocked.' He laughed shortly, adopting his customary stance of feet apart, hands in his pockets. 'This family never waits for explanations, it just jumps to conclusions and condemns out of hand.' It was as bitter a speech as she had ever heard from him and she felt sure that more than the present incident had provoked it.

'I—I had a fall,' Mora explained. 'Adam pulled me out of the snow and—well, as you can see, I'm not much the worse for it, but I could have been.'

Hamish hesitated briefly, seeming to notice for the first time her damp hair and clothes. 'I had a phone call,' he said at last. 'Helen rang to say that she was afraid you might take the path round by the loch and she was worried.'

Mora stared at him, conscious of Adam's gaze fixed on her curiously. 'What was worrying her?' Adam asked. 'Why did she think Mora might come to grief?'

'She said there was a deep drift over the hollow by the shieling and she was afraid Mora might have an accident.' He frowned at Mora disapprovingly. 'It seems she was right,' he said shortly. 'You *wouldn't* listen to reason.'

'Wouldn't listen to——' Mora shook her head, her eyes wide, stunned by the other girl's cunning. 'But she made no mention of the drift to me. She told me the path was clear and—and more or less dared me to come back this way.'

'Dared you?' Hamish looked unconvinced. 'But, Mora, surely you must have misunderstood. Helen warned you about the drift and tried to talk you out of going that way, but you were stubborn and refused to be put off.'

'And you believed her?' Mora accused. 'Because you think I'm stubborn.'

'You can't resist a challenge, I know that,' Hamish amended. 'It sounds quite logical to me, knowing Helen and knowing you.'

'You don't *know* either of us, apparently,' she said crossly. 'She said nothing to me about the drift or I'd have been on the look-out for it. I'm not an idiot, Hamish.'

'I'm not suggesting you are,' he retorted. 'But you *are* obstinate, and I remember only a couple of nights ago when you insisted on going to the tower room, just because Adam had dared you to.' Adam's deep chuckle recalled them both and Hamish looked embarrassed. 'I'm sorry, Mora, I should be more concerned with you than your motives. Are you hurt?'

'She's wet and cold and frightened,' Adam informed him before Mora could speak for herself. 'I've performed a little therapy with warmth and——' He arched his brows expressively as a substitute for the last word and Mora saw the dark flush colour Hamish's face from neck to brow as it did when he was in danger of losing his temper. 'I suggest you get her home and into something dry and warm,' Adam added, apparently unconcerned by the approaching storm. 'I can't bring her, because Klonda's hurt a leg and I shall have to walk him home.'

'I wouldn't let you touch her again,' said Hamish, his voice taut and sharp with anger. 'I'll take care of her from now on.'

'Well, just make sure you do,' Adam told him lightly, 'or you may find there's someone else willing to do it for you.'

CHAPTER NINE

AFTER the incident at the shieling, when she and Hamish
had so nearly quarrelled over Helen Murdoe's warning, or
lack of it, Mora found her position at Glen Ghyll more
uncomfortable than at any time since she had arrived nearly
three months before. Fergus and Tizzy and the newest
McLean had gone home to Glen Isla, and Sir James,
Hamish and Miss Alison McLean now comprised the entire
household.

Sir James was a considerate, even indulgent, employer
and there was little for her to do, but he seemed to enjoy
having her around and she rode with him several times,
though she found him a hard and courageous rider who set
a pace that she found difficult to match. It was Hamish who
made her life less than easy with his almost insane jealousy.

If ever Adam was in the castle, Hamish made sure that
he and Mora were never alone together, even, if possible,
preventing conversation between them, until Mora found
her patience growing short. Adam, on the other hand,
seemed to find the situation amusing, and his mockery and
laughter when he saw how his brother's manner annoyed
her did nothing to soothe her temper.

She still managed, sometimes, to walk or ride alone,
because Hamish was so often busy, but now that he was
involved with the family business, Adam was usually just as
busy, so that there was no need for him to worry that they
might be together. The situation, Mora felt, was rapidly
becoming intolerable and she must soon do something about
it.

It was some three or four weeks into the new year and

Mora was going into her room one evening after dinner. Something caught her eye as she opened the door and she frowned curiously, turning her head to look over her right shoulder. It had been no more than a slight flutter of movement at the corner of the corridor into the north wing and a soft whisper of sound, as if someone moved.

The family were still downstairs, she knew, and it was because Helen Murdoe was a dinner guest that Mora had excused herself as soon as she politely could and come to her room, so who could be moving about in the north wing?

For a second of indecision she stared along the length of the corridor, a tingle of excitement trickling along her spine, then she left her door half open and went, light-footed, along the carpeted way to the north wing.

Just before she reached the corner, she slowed her already slow walk and felt idiotically like a burglar as she trod cautiously and silently to the turn in the corridor, almost jumping out of her skin when she saw a figure standing there in the semi-darkness.

The lights in the north corridor had not be switched on and only the diffused light from behind her showed the tall, shadowy shape of a man standing there so still he might almost have been a statue.

She caught her breath, her lips parted, eyes wide, half fearful, half excited as she stared at him, looking like a rather lovely ghost herself in the full pale dress she wore and with her softly curling hair brushed upwards and held by a wide band. She stood as breathlessly still as he did, and then a deep chuckle dispelled her momentary illusion of the first Adam McLean and she released her breath in a long sigh.

'You really believed it for a moment, didn't you?' Adam teased her.

'Of course I didn't,' she denied, her cheeks flushed at the way she had been fooled. 'I knew it was you.'

He arched a querying brow at her. 'Is that why you

came?' he asked, and chuckled when he saw from her face that she realised the trap she had been led into. He moved only when she went to turn away, touching her arm and turning her back towards him. 'Don't go, Mora.'

She hesitated, uncertain of herself and of him. 'I don't know why I came,' she said. 'I—I was curious, I think. I saw a movement and heard a sound of—of——' She fluttered her hands in soundless explanation.

'I knew you'd be unable to resist it if you thought my disreputable namesake was on the prowl,' he said, and his eyes swept over her face in swift appraisal, watching her expression as well he could in the treacherous light from behind her. 'Most girls would have run away—but not you. I knew you'd come and investigate.'

She stood with his hand holding her arm, the telltale pulse throbbing wildly in her temple. 'I presume you had a reason for getting me here,' she said, trying to sound matter-of-fact, and he smiled.

'Of course,' he admitted, and added with a grin, 'but not the obvious one, although Hamish would never believe it.'

She glanced uneasily over her shoulder at the mention of his brother. 'I—I don't know that I should be here like this,' she said. 'It seems an odd way to behave to me.'

'It needs to be with Hamish always standing guard on you,' he retorted. 'I wanted to see you alone and it's been impossible with Hamish always with you and watching you like a hawk; this was my only chance. With Helen coming to dinner I guessed you'd be leaving the party as soon as you could. In fact I banked on it.'

'I wish I knew just what you're up to,' Mora said doubtfully. 'Why do you want to see me? And why do you have to behave as if I'm not a free agent? Hamish doesn't watch me all the time, you're doing him an injustice.'

'No?' He laughed shortly. 'He's never let you out of his sight when I'm around since he came looking for you and found us together in the shieling, now has he?'

129

'Of course he has,' she averred uneasily, conscious of his watching eyes. 'I've been out any number of times on my own and with Sir James.'

He chuckled darkly. 'Only when he knew I was too occupied to be able to speak to you,' he insisted. 'Anyway, I've managed it at last.'

'I don't understand you,' said Mora, wishing she had resisted the temptation to seek out the origin of the movement that had attracted her to the north wing. 'Does anyone know you're here—in the castle, I mean?'

'No. But I don't *have* to ask permission before I come here, you know.'

'I didn't mean that,' she murmured hastily. 'I just wondered——'

'Don't worry,' he interrupted. 'Hamish won't know if you don't tell him.'

She flushed at the implication that Hamish was the reason for her doubt and felt the familiar anger tinge her cheeks pink. 'I don't have to account to Hamish for my actions,' she told him shortly. 'I work for your father, not Hamish.'

His laugh sounded deep and quiet down the long dark corridor. 'Father keeps you here because he hopes you will eventually marry Hamish,' he said with assurance. 'That secretary business is only a blind, and well you know it.'

'I *do* work for Sir James,' she protested, though she knew he was more than half right about his father's reason for employing her.

'You play at secretary,' he taunted, 'until Hamish manages to win you round. That's the whole idea behind it.'

'Oh, you know so much!' she said crossly. 'And if you've only inveigled me along here to be nasty about Hamish, I'm going.' As good as her word, she would have moved away, but he still had his hand on her arm, and she hesitated to snatch it away.

'I didn't,' he informed her, suddenly sober again. 'I

wanted you to come along to Grandfather's room with me if you would.' He looked down at the few inches of carpet between their feet, uncharacteristically hesitant. 'There's something—some things I'd like you to see. He left me a lot of things that I shall never have any use for, but you may like to have them. There's only one point—I'd rather the rest of the family didn't know about it.'

She stared at him for a moment, uncertainly, her eyes trying to see his face in the soft almost dark. 'I—I don't quite understand,' she demurred, wishing the throb of her pulse would subside and enable her to think more clearly. 'If it's family business surely they have more right to know about it than I have.'

He sighed his exasperation and she was reminded of the first time she had seen him on the stairs, beside the portrait of the first Adam. 'Oh, will you stop havering, woman, and come if you're coming.' That first time she had refused to accompany him when he had urged her with almost the same words. This time she hesitated only briefly, then nodded silent agreement and followed him to the room that had been Ian McLean's.

He reached in a hand and turned on the lights and she found her gaze instinctively going to the empty chair beside the window. 'Nothing's changed,' she said, voicing her surprise that the room looked exactly the same as before, and he smiled.

'It will soon,' he told her. 'Now that all the legal formalities are settled, Ramsey and I can set to and sort out these two rooms. This one and the old man's bedroom.' He pulled an old-fashioned leather jewel case from a cupboard in the corner, a broad deep case with the initials 'M.J.McL.' on the lid. 'Mary Jean McLean,' he explained, seeing her curious eyes. 'My grandmother.' He laid the case on a table and seemed once again to be unusually indeterminate.

'She's—dead, too?' Mora asked, and he nodded.

'She died when my aunt was born and the old man never married again.' He unlocked the case as he spoke and stood for a moment staring down at the contents as if he was still undecided what he should do about them. 'There were a lot of things, as I said, Mora, that the old man left to me which—well, I wish he hadn't, but there's nothing I can do about that now except what I think he would have approved of.' He called her over and she answered the beckoning finger with a strange feeling of excitement in her heart, her eyes on his face curiously.

The top tray of the case was lined with red velvet, now faded and tired-looking, but on it lay a cascade of light and colour that glittered and shone in the overhead light and Mora gazed at it for a moment in awed silence. 'There must be a fortune there,' she whispered at last, and he shrugged.

'Possibly there is,' he said carelessly. 'I'm never very impressed with the stuff; beautiful women don't need trimming up and plain ones only look worse when they wear jewels. It was my grandmother's, and the old man must have kept it all these years without it seeing the light of day—at least I've never seen anyone wearing it. Now he's left it to me.' Something in his voice made her raise her eyes and look at him—some trace of wistfulness that had, at times, coloured his grandfather's voice, and she felt the pulse in her temple throb dizzily when he met her gaze. 'I thought you might like it as you were so fond of the old man.'

She stared at him for a moment unbelievingly. 'But, Adam, I—I couldn't. I couldn't possibly.' Her voice trembled and threatened to break and the way he was looking at her did nothing to help her self-control. 'Your grandfather must have—must have had a reason for leaving it all to you. You can't just give it all away to—to anyone.' She thought she knew the purpose of the old man's gift and her mind raced as she wondered at Adam's giving it to her.

'I know what his reason was,' Adam said wryly, 'but since I can't see myself ever having a wife, in the foreseeable future anyway, I'd rather you had it.' He smiled at her,

132

his mouth tilted crookedly, giving him a look which was both impudent and appealing and which set her heart thumping uneasily hard against her ribs. 'Call it a dowry for when you marry Hamish,' he told her. 'No one need ever know where it came from, it's improbable that anyone in the family has seen it, so there's no chance of them recognising it. They'll be none the wiser unless you tell them.'

'But *I* shall know,' she insisted. 'And if I don't marry Hamish——'

'If you don't,' he interrupted shortly, 'he's a bigger fool than I took him for and less of a McLean than I gave him credit for.'

'I don't want to marry him, Adam!' Her protest sounded like a plea, and for a moment he gazed at her with an intensity that she found hard to bear, then he laughed.

'Oh, you'll marry him,' he assured her. 'Hamish is pretty good at getting his own way.'

'Aren't you?' she retorted, and saw him smile.

'Not always,' he admitted, 'but you'll take these trinkets because I want you to, won't you?'

'No! I can't, Adam. And don't be so sure that you'll never marry.' She looked at him curiously, her thoughts with Helen Murdoe and her ambitions that so obviously included Adam. Helen Murdoe, she thought, would have other ideas about his remaining single, and she was not a girl to be easily dissuaded.

The old familiar mockery glittered in his eyes as he looked at her briefly before walking across to the window to look down into the darkness below. 'The first Adam never married, you know, he was too busy with—other matters to find himself a wife.'

'Well, you're not the first Adam,' she said shortly, annoyed with herself because she felt so near to tears and could find no reasonable excuse for them. 'You should stop modelling yourself on him and start living your own life.'

'I intend to as from next month,' he informed her, and

133

she felt a prickle of apprehension when she looked across the room at him. 'I'm leaving for Canada at the end of February.'

She knew she was staring at him, that her eyes were wide with surprise and her mouth partly open to speak words that refused to form. 'Canada?'

'That's right.' He laughed shortly, looking at her reflection in the window. 'What's the matter; isn't it far enough away for you?'

'But why? What about——?' She had almost referred to Richie as his son, but she could not bring herself to let him know that his secret was known to her and he misread her intention.

'Helen?' he asked, and laughed. 'Helen won't weep over me for very long, Mora, don't worry.'

'She—she still loves you,' Mora ventured hesitantly, and saw his brows arch in surprise, turning to look at her.

'Helen does? I doubt it—it's the thought of Glen Ghyll that Helen loves, not me.'

She looked puzzled. 'I don't understand.'

He frowned for a moment as if he doubted her bewilderment was genuine. 'Are you telling me that you still think Hamish is the eldest brother? Hasn't he enlightened you yet? Hasn't he used it as bait to get you to marry him?' She flushed at the last question and bit her lip when he laughed softly. 'He's sharper than I thought, but it hasn't helped him much so far, has it?'

'If you mean has he deliberately let me believe he's the heir to—to all this so that it will influence me in his favour, you're wrong!' Her voice trembled, not only in anger but because he should think it possible that she could be influenced in that way. 'Hamish knows I'm not as mercenary as that—I thought you did.'

He turned from her suddenly. His back to the lighted room, his forehead pressed against the cool glass of the window and the reflected features she saw were sober and contrite. 'I'm sorry,' he said quietly, at last, lifting his head

134

and looking at her over his shoulder.

She shook her head. 'It doesn't matter.'

'Doesn't it? Not to discover that *I'm* the poor devil who inherits all the hundred and one problems that go with a place like Glen Ghyll? I seem to remember that you expressed pity for Hamish when you thought it was his problem.'

'Then I have pity for you—for the same reason,' she said softly. 'But if Glen Ghyll is to be yours, why don't you stay here and help to run it now? Why run away to Canada?'

He turned round to face her, taking up the familiar stance, and she crossed the room to stand near him, some unbidden throb of excitement urging her on when she knew she should have turned and gone. 'Running away?' he echoed. 'Is that how it looks?'

'*Isn't* it?' she asked. 'You could stay and help here. You own the biggest share of the business now and if the estate is to be yours too, you *should* stay. Why are you running away, Adam?'

He looked down at her flushed cheeks and wide blue eyes for a long moment, his gaze deep and searching, then he shook his head slowly. 'Because history has a habit of repeating itself in this family,' he said, 'and I've done my share of disrupting other people's lives already.'

There seemed to be no answer to that and she could only stand there, looking very still and rather forlorn in her pale dress and with her hands clasped in front of her. 'It's such a long way,' she managed at last, and raised her eyes to see him move a step nearer before his arms went round her, strong and possessive, and his mouth covered her half-hearted protest and stilled it.

It seemed an eternity before she breathed again and he was standing over near the big desk, putting a key into the lock of the jewellery case. 'You'd better put this somewhere safe,' he said, and sounded so matter-of-fact that she stared at him for a moment in silence. 'Keep it locked,' he went on, 'and put the bits and pieces into a different case when

135

you can, in case Hamish sees it.'

'I—I can't take them, Adam.' She stood beside him, her hands trembling as she put them behind her, in a childish gesture of refusal, when he offered her the key.

'If you don't have them no one will,' he said quietly. 'I'll put them away somewhere in this vast heap and they can stay lost until some future McLean unearths them and presents them to his bride.'

'Please, Adam.' He shook his head adamantly and she reluctantly held out her hand for the key.

'Keep them safe,' he warned her softly as he closed her fingers over the key and bent his head to kiss her gently beside her mouth.

Fergus's baby son was christened on the last day of January and the young family came back to Glen Ghyll afterwards for a celebration drink. 'To the latest McLean.' Sir James raised his glass. 'May he prosper, but honestly.'

'The first grandson,' Fergus said with a satisfied smile at his sleeping son, and Mora glanced up hastily at Hamish.

'The first grandson,' Hamish echoed, and the words were repeated by them all, even Mora, whose image for the toast was a dark, grey-eyed little boy of nearly five, who loved playing by the burn.

Perhaps it was the thought of Richie that sent her down the familiar path, a couple of days later, towards the stream, now swollen with the first of February's rain. The clouds had cleared for the moment and it was warmer than of late, though still cold enough to need plenty of warm clothing.

She could hear the sound of the water rushing over the stones long before she got near enough to see it and she realised that the last two days would have turned it from a gently flowing stream into a fast running torrent as it rushed down from the hills behind Glencairn, fed on its way by the melting snow.

She approached Effie Smith's cottage and, seeing her from the window, Richie came running out, his face as usual beaming a welcome so that she felt, not for the first time, a tinge of pity for the rather lonely life he led.

'Can I come, Mora?' he pleaded. 'Can I?'

Effie Smith appeared in the doorway, smiling indulgently, no longer hesitant as she had been that first time. 'May he come, Mrs. Smith?' Mora asked. 'Just as far as the burn and back.'

'If ye dinnae mind takin' him,' Effie Smith agreed. 'He's no much trouble usually, but a couple o' days inside an' he's likely ta drive me daft wi' his worryin'.'

Mora laughed as Richie struggled into his wellington boots, his small face flushed with the effort. He wore nothing on his head and Mora thought how like Adam he looked with his dark hair falling across his forehead, his grey eyes dancing with mischief. 'We'll have to go carefully down here,' Mora warned him as they approached the stream. 'The burn's in flood and it could be dangerous.'

'I'm going to Can'da,' Richie announced, ignoring the warning and racing on ahead, calling the information over his shoulder as he ran.

'Richie! Come back!' He must have sensed her fear for him, for he came back immediately to rejoin her, taking her hand as if to reassure her and again reminded her of Adam. 'Do you want to go to Canada?' she asked, and he frowned thoughtfully.

'I don't know,' he said cautiously. 'It's nice here.'

'It is,' she agreed. 'But I believe Canada is very like Scotland in places, so you won't feel too homesick.'

'Homesick?' He looked at her curiously.

'It's when you have—a sort of feeling that you'd like to go back home,' she explained. 'A sort of sad feeling.'

'Oh.' He looked doubtful, then cheered almost immediately. 'Adam says it's nice in Can'da too,' he told her in that oddly grown up way he had, and she smiled.

'Then I'm sure he's right,' she said, smiling down at the solemnity of the little face. 'You'll have snow for much longer in Canada too. They have very deep snow for a long time.'

He frowned as if he found that information less pleasing. 'A long time?'

'Mm. Much longer than we have it here. Why?' she added, 'don't you like snow?'

'Not when I have to stay in,' he retorted, and she laughed. There was something refreshingly honest about Richie that she found irresistible and for a moment she felt an overwhelming pity for him that he should be denied a normal family upbringing. He should be entitled to have at least as much fuss made of him as Fergus's baby son and not treated like an outcast because Adam had never married his mother.

For the moment, however, Richie seemed unconcerned with his lack of home life and was content to explore the world as he found it. The stream, as usual, proved an unfailing source of delight and the deeper, swifter water made it even more attractive.

'Don't go in, Richie,' Mora warned him, keeping a wary eye on his activities. 'Stay on the bank or you'll come to grief.'

'It's deep,' Richie informed her, using a stick as a measuring gauge.

'I know it's deep; too deep to go wading in,' Mora told him, 'so stay out of it.'

'I will,' he assured her, and she smiled at his self-confidence. 'Adam's coming,' he added a moment later, and she looked over her shoulder expecting to see him.

'Not *yet*,' Richie went on. 'But he always comes on—on——'

'Tuesdays?' Mora guessed, and he nodded.

'Yes. Effie says he does. He stops longer on Tuesdays.'

'I see. Well, perhaps we'd better go back now in case he wonders where you are.'

He grinned over one shoulder at her, knowingly. 'He'll come,' he informed her, and turned back to his latest exploit, while Mora watched him, uncertain whether or not she wanted to see Adam again after their last meeting.

She was given no time to decide, for a moment later Richie gave his usual cry of welcome and came sploshing his way up from the bank, with a beaming smile on his face. Adam reined in the big black and dismounted in time to catch the body hurtling towards him, shrieking a welcome.

'Whoa!' Adam laughed. 'You'll split my eardrums if you go on like that!' He glanced up at Mora, following more slowly, and his smile had a trace of uncertainty she had never seen there before. 'Hello, Mora, have you been voted nursemaid again?'

'I don't mind,' she said, responding to the smile. 'He's no trouble and very obedient.'

'Well trained,' he said with a glint of the old mockery in his eyes. 'A big stick and a tight rein.'

'I don't believe it,' Mora laughed, shaking her head. 'Not Richie, he's too happy, and he's never been cowed in his life, I'm sure.'

His face sobered suddenly, as if the words recalled something he had for a moment forgotten, and he held the boy against him briefly, his eyes hard. 'He was once when he was very small,' he said shortly, 'but never again while I have anything to do with it, whatever the family think.' And Mora thought the challenge in the grey eyes was directed as much at her as at Hamish or any of the rest of his family.

CHAPTER TEN

THE weather turned so much worse for the next few days
that Mora had not ventured out, even for a short walk. The
once gently ambling stream had become a rushing torrent,
splashing over the stones with a gabble of sound that could
be heard several yards away; fed by the melting snow and
the almost ceaseless rain of the last few days. The narrow
road to Glencairn was dotted with so many puddles that it
was impossible to avoid them and everywhere the trees and
scrub dripped dismally in the persistent drizzle.

It was Sunday afternoon and Fergus and Tizzy, with
their baby son, had joined the family for lunch as was usual.
Only Hamish was missing, at the moment, having gone into
the study-cum-office, to make a telephone call about some
matter that was too important even to wait for Monday
morning, apparently.

Mora sat on the wide window-seat, one foot curled under
her, gazing hopefully out at the now gradually diminishing
rain. Perhaps by this evening it would be fine enough to
venture at least as far as the courtyard for a breath of fresh
air.

The murmur of voices behind her made little impression
on her absent thoughts as she gazed out of the window and
she was aware only of an air of tranquillity in the big room,
with the crackling fire burning in the huge fireplace and the
easy familiarity of family conversation. It was only when
the door opened with rather more than usual suddenness
that she was jolted out of her reverie and turned startled
eyes as Hamish came into the room.

He wore a worried frown between his brows and his grey

eyes were dark with some emotion that Mora could not even guess at. Seeing him, Sir James got up from his arm-chair hastily, his fierce blue eyes narrowed curiously as he looked at his son's face. 'Hamish? What the devil's the matter? Is someone hurt?' He sent a hasty, reassuring glance round his family. 'Adam?'

Hamish shook his head. 'It's the boy—Richie.'

Mora heard her own breath sharply indrawn and she uncurled herself on the window-seat, her eyes on Hamish's face, trying to read from his expression what had happened, but in vain. 'What's happened?' Sir James asked, his tone reflecting her own impatience.

Hamish ran a hand through the thickness of his hair. 'No one knows for sure,' he said. 'The boy's missing.'

'Missing?' Sir James echoed the brief answer. 'But how? Where?'

Hamish flicked a glance at Mora before answering, his expression almost apologetic, she thought. 'You know that Adam always has the boy with him all day on Sundays?' Sir James nodded. 'It seems that Adam left him for a few minutes, he had to go and see Ramsey about something in the kitchen and the boy—Richie—must have slipped out while he was gone.'

Sir James looked fiercely disbelieving, his bright blue eyes narrowed. 'But how the devil could the child have got far enough to be lost in only a few minutes?' he asked.

'Apparently Richie was playing in one of the bedrooms,' Hamish answered. 'He wasn't actually in the same room as Adam so that he didn't realise immediately that he was missing. In fact he'd been back some time and he suddenly realised that he couldn't hear him any longer and called to him, then went into the bedroom to look for him. He wasn't there.'

'There's something wrong somewhere,' Sir James opined. 'Where's Adam?'

'Out looking for the boy,' Hamish said. 'Ramsey rang Nana to tell her what had happened and she caught me as I

141

was on my way back in here.'

'How long as he been gone?' Sir James asked, and Mora heard their voices only vaguely above the rapid and sickening thud of her heart, remembering how Richie hated to be kept in whenever the weather was bad as it had been for the last few days.

'About an hour or more altogether,' said Hamish. 'Ramsey thought he'd better let someone know, he's worried about the boy and about Adam.'

'Has he been over to the Smiths to see if he's there?' It was Fergus who asked, and his voice as well as his face expressed the concern he made no attempt to hide.

Hamish nodded. 'It was the first place they tried, but he wasn't there and they haven't seen anything of him. It all took time, of course, it must be getting on for a couple of hours now since he went.'

'As long as that?' Sir James exclaimed, and Hamish nodded.

'Ramsey reckoned that Adam was with him about five minutes or so and it was nearly half an hour before Adam missed him, then they looked around in the cottage first to make sure he wasn't hiding from them. It's something he often does for fun, apparently. Then they went to Smiths' and asked there, it was getting on for an hour before they started to look for him outside.'

'And we've only just been told,' Sir James said, almost as if he spoke to himself, his broad, usually cheerful face sober and worried-looking.

'The burn!' It was Mora's voice that broke the ensuing silence and she was on her feet, moved at last by the need for action. 'He'll be down by the burn somewhere, playing with the water, it's almost certain. I know Richie—that's where he'll be!'

She felt all eyes turned on her and the colour rose in her cheeks at the mingled curiosity and surprise she saw there.

'The burn's in flood,' Sir James said flatly. 'A child of only five too near that water——' He did not finish the sentence, but Mora heard Tizzy's sharp intake of breath.

'*Does* he play near the burn, Mora?' Sir James asked, his fierce eyes dulled by the prospect that faced them.

Mora nodded. 'Always when he has the chance,' she replied. 'I take him there myself quite often when it's fine—he loves it.'

'You know him that well?' Even now Hamish could find time to inject a note of disapproval into his voice as he looked at her, and she shook her head as she walked across the room towards the door, her eyes shiny with impatience and anger.

'I know him well enough to care that he may be in danger,' she retorted, tossing her head as she passed Hamish. 'And I'm going to help Adam look for him, since no one else seems to be going to.'

She realised, as she closed the door behind her, that she had been unforgivably rude and perhaps unfair in her condemnation, but the thought uppermost in her mind was Richie's danger and the agony of mind that Adam must be going through.

By the time she came downstairs again, clothed for the outdoors, Hamish and Fergus were already leaving by the front door, clad in rubber boots and mackintoshes. Hamish turned as she joined them, his eyes dark and reproachful.

'Father is following us in a minute or two,' he told her. 'It may be a long job if the boy's gone far and he's had plenty of time to have got himself thoroughly lost by now. I had every intention of helping Adam look for him,' he added, and she put a conciliatory hand on his arm as they went down the steps on to the squelching wet gravel of the driveway.

'I know,' she said contritely. 'I'm sorry, Hamish, I shouldn't have spoken as I did.' She looked past him to his brother, grim-faced and dour. 'Fergus, I must apologise to you too. I didn't really mean it, I was just so worried about Richie. He's such a nice little boy, and the thought of what might have happened to him, I——'

143

Fergus's grey eyes, so like Hamish's, turned on her briefly, deep and meaningful, and the wide mouth smiled at her wryly. 'Please don't apologise, Mora, I understand how you feel,' he told her, and for some inexplicable reason she felt the colour rush into her cheeks as she lowered her eyes.

The ground was thickly muddy under foot and already, as they went down the path by the Smiths' cottage, they could hear the rapid, chilling sound of the water rushing along over the stony bed of the stream. 'We'll see if the Smiths are around first,' Hamish said as they came alongside the little cottage. 'There may be some news.'

The door of the cottage was ajar, but a call brought no response, so presumably the Smiths were out looking for Richie as well. 'We'd best split up,' Fergus decreed. 'There's no point in staying in a bunch as we are and we'll have to take a chance on covering the same ground twice.' He looked around him with the air of hopelessness that many must feel at the start of such a search. 'The boy could be anywhere. I'll look among this scrub this side, it's easy to get lost in there when you're only small and can't see over the top of it. I remember I was lost in there myself once and I was terrified.'

'And you were a bit older than five,' Hamish remarked grimly, his eyes dark with worry as he looked over at the thick, bare scrub, still dripping wet, although the drizzle had now ceased. 'I'll take the bank along this way.' He waved his left arm in a wide sweep. 'Heaven knows where Adam and the others are.' He looked down at Mora's tight, cold face and put a comforting hand on her arm. 'We'll find him, Mora, don't worry. From what I've seen of him he's a sturdy child, he shouldn't come to much harm as long as he's stayed away from the burn.'

Mora raised unhappy eyes to him, shaking her head. 'He won't have,' she said with certainty. 'He'll be somewhere near the water, Hamish, I know it. He wouldn't be able to resist the water, he loves it and—and he's enough like Adam

144

to follow his own inclinations, regardless of the consequences.'

'We'll find him,' he repeated. 'Why don't you go back and wait?'

She shook her head, her eyes misty bright with tears. 'I, can't,' she whispered. 'I just can't wait, Hamish, I must help.' She turned and looked along the other bank of the stream as it wound towards Glencairn. 'I'll go along this way and look for him.'

Hamish looked doubtful at the prospect, but he made no protest, only put an arm round her shoulders and gave them a brief, consoling hug. 'Be careful,' he warned. 'The ground's pretty treacherous. Don't go too near the water in case you slip.'

'I'll be careful,' she promised with a wan smile. 'I always am now.' Indeed, since she had been so nearly suffocated in that deep snowdrift by the shieling, she had learned to treat this beautiful but at times dangerous country with more respect.

It was hard, slow going with the ground sucking muddily at her boots as she walked, and always the loud, gabbling voice of the burn reminded her of what she might find if Richie had ventured too near to it.

It was a prospect she tried not to dwell on, but there was no escaping the fact that Richie would almost inevitably have escaped from under Adam's watchful eye to seek the irresistible fascination of the running water. He was an adventurous child and usually obedient but, as she had told Hamish, he was too much like Adam to be able to resist the opportunity that Adam's temporary absence had offered him, and his enforced confinement during the last few days must have chafed his restless spirit.

No scrub-bush escaped her attention and she called the boy's name every few feet, in case he should be within hearing and able to answer, but no answering voice hailed her and her hopes sank lower and lower as she went on.

Her fingers were chilled even in their warm gloves and

145

the coldness of the wet ground penetrated her boots as she squelched along the bank, searching, her eyes at times seeing movement that turned out to be only the wind stirring the scrub into action.

The short winter afternoon was already drawing in and she had walked almost as far as the beginning of the loch when she received, at last, a reply to her anxious calling. 'Mora?' She jerked her head round sharply in the direction of the voice and emerged a second later from behind the bare, snagging branches of a bush, to see Adam standing there.

'Adam, you——' She saw then that he was alone and her heart sank until she could barely hold back the tears that gave her a deceptively bright-eyed look.

The deep grey eyes looked at her for a moment almost angrily. 'What in heaven's name are *you* doing here?' he asked.

'I—I came to help look for Richie,' she told him, her eyes on the drawn, grey look of his face and the tightness of his mouth. He wore no topcoat and mud spattered his clothes; his hands, ungloved, were scratched where he had pulled aside the bushes in his search for the boy.

'You could have landed your*self* in trouble,' he said shortly. 'Are you alone?'

She shook her head. 'No, not really. Hamish and Fergus have gone along the other side of the bank and your father is out looking too.'

For a moment a trace of mockery lit the dark face and twisted his mouth into a bitter smile. 'Imagine that,' he said. 'All hands to the pumps—to find Richie.'

'Of course—what else did you expect?' Mora asked shortly, forgetting her own unfortunate remark earlier.

He made no answer, but shook his head as if he regretted his words as much as she had done her own. 'You'd better stick with me,' he told her. 'Hamish should have had more sense than to let you come on your own.'

'He had no choice,' Mora retorted as they set off along

146

the bank again. 'I intended coming, and nothing Hamish could have said would have stopped me.'

'You wouldn't have done,' Adam murmured darkly,' if you belonged to me.' Mora forbore to make the obvious retort about Richie but sent him a look from under her long lashes that was not without speculation.

They were nearly to the loch by now and the wide, dark expanse of water looked even more than usually ominous under the overcast skies, so that Mora shuddered involuntarily. They walked some distance apart, moving every bush and looking behind every wind-stunted tree, the overcast and the shortening daylight playing cruel tricks on their eyes as they searched.

'Richie!' She called again as she had done all the way along and, after only a brief pause, Adam's voice cried out from beside one of the bushes.

'Mora, here!'

She turned sharply towards the cry, her heart hammering unmercifully hard against her ribs and a silent prayer on her lips as she ran the few few feet to join him. 'Adam——!' The word sounded harsh in her throat as she looked down to see him knelt beside the boy, holding him cradled in his arms.

'He's all right,' he assured her, relief flooding the dark face as he lifted the child and looked down at the muddy, tear-stained face against his chest.

'Oh, thank God!' Mora whispered, her throat so constricted that she almost choked on the words.

Adam rested his face briefly against the dark wet head, his eyes glinting in the dying light. 'I'll give him the hiding of his life when I get him home,' he said huskily.

Mora, convinced he would do no such thing, laughed her relief, the tears that had threatened for so long rolling warmly down her cheeks unchecked as she looked at them both. 'Let's get him home first,' she said. Richie made no move as they walked back along the muddy bank of the burn, but he murmured sleepily when Adam wrapped him in his jacket. 'Are you *sure* he's all right?' she asked after a moment or two.

'He's fine,' Adam assured her. 'He's dirty and tired and he's probably playing possum so that he won't get his just deserts. Undoubtedly he'll be hungry—he usually is.'

Mora laughed, her relief making her feel quite light-headed. 'Small boys usually are, aren't they?'

'I don't know, are they?' The old challenging gleam met her eyes when she turned her head and she thought that the immense feeling of relief they both felt was making them both a little crazy at the moment.

'Well, aren't they?'

'I've never had much to do with children until this young man,' he confessed, 'so my experience is limited.'

'Mine's even more limited,' she retorted. 'I never *was* a little boy, and you must have been at some time, surely.' She felt her colour rise betrayingly under his scrutiny. 'I can only go by hearsay, that's all.'

'Oh, I see,' he said solemnly. 'I thought perhaps you had a husband and family tucked away somewhere.'

She bit on the retort that rose to her lips and instead wrinkled her nose at him in an expression of reproach. 'We'd better keep a look out for the rest of the search party,' she said.

They walked in silence for several moments, with no sign of the others anywhere to be seen, then he turned his head and looked at her with a curious intensity, as if he debated the wisdom of what he was about to say. 'Do you remember what you said to me a few days ago, in Grandfather McLean's room?' he asked suddenly, and she looked briefly startled at the unexpectedness of the question, then nodded, conscious of the throbbing pulse in her temple as she remembered the meeting he referred to only too well, though which particular part of their conversation he meant she had no idea, as yet.

'I—I remember we—we talked,' she admitted cautiously, trying not to look at him as she spoke for fear of meeting his eyes again.

He smiled wryly. 'You offered me some advice,' he said. 'In fact you *told* me what I should do.' He turned his head again and looked down at her so that she felt herself compelled to look at him, however briefly. '*Do* you think I should stay on here—at Glen Ghyll?' So that was it! He was evidently having second thoughts about leaving Glen Ghyll again, or perhaps Richie had told him that he did not want to go. He would take the boy's feelings into consideration, she thought.

'I—I don't know.' She hesitated to be as adamant again as she had been then. Telling him that he should stay and look after his inheritance had seemed easy then, now it seemed so much more important to say the right thing, though she could not imagine why. Nothing had changed, but it seemed an unfair question to put to her; something he should have decided for himself before now.

'You seemed pretty sure then,' he said, with a trace of the impatience he frequently showed when she hesitated over answering him. She lifted her chin at the note of challenge, her eyes bright. 'Very well—I'm sure now. I think you should stay on here.'

'Why?' She blinked at the brief, frankly curious question.

'Why, because—because you should,' she said, hesitating to use the hackneyed word 'duty', though she knew from his expression that he guessed her intention.

'Because it's my duty as the eldest son?' he asked dryly, and she flushed, a challenge in her eyes.

'Yes—if you care to put it like that.'

He drew a deep breath and looked at her with an intensity she found disturbing. 'And that's the only reason?'

She did not answer at once, but looked down at the muddy ground they were walking over, a flutter of dark lashes betraying her uncertainty. 'It's a good enough reason, isn't it?' she asked, and he laughed softly.

'Good enough for now,' he agreed, and looked down at

the sleepy face of the boy. 'I hope you won't mind not going to Canada, Richie,' he said softly. 'But I don't think you will somehow.'

'But you don't mean——' Mora began, her eyes wide with disbelief. 'Adam, you can't just change your plans like that—because I——'

'It's settled,' he interrupted cheerfully. 'We don't go to Canada, we stay here.'

'But I didn't mean you to act so rashly on my opinion,' she objected. 'It's a big decision, Adam.'

'I know,' he agreed. 'I've given it a great deal of thought, and now you've given the idea your O.K., that settles it. We stay, though I don't think the family are going to take kindly to the change of plan. Especially Hamish,' he added, with a wry glance in her direction.

They walked in silence for a while, Mora's mind spinning busily with the suddenness of it all. 'I wish,' she said at last, 'that you hadn't—hadn't thrown the onus of decision on to me, Adam. It wasn't really fair.'

He arched his brows, laughing shortly at her objection. 'I think it was,' he said, and added with a grin, 'It's too late to change your mind now.'

They found the Smiths, with Hamish and Fergus, standing disconsolately at the end of the path in company with Sir James, as they came round the last bend and all five faces looked across at them anxiously so that Mora left Adam and ran as best she could along the muddy bank to tell them the good news.

'He's quite all right,' she said a little breathlessly, addressing herself to Sir James, and she saw the broad face flood with relief. Hamish put an arm round her shoulders and hugged her to him.

'Thank God for that,' he murmured, and the sincerity in the words gave her immense satisfaction, for it was obvious that whatever their feelings about the boy had been, their relief at his safety was genuine enough.

Armed with the news, the Smiths discreetly withdrew

150

from the family circle and moved across to meet Ramsey coming along the opposite path, his dark face wrinkled and anxious.

Adam joined Mora and his family, Richie stirring sleepily as the sound of other voices disturbed him, his eyes seeking out Mora as the one familiar face, apart from Adam, from the strange ones that surrounded him. He looked around at the others, uncertain and wearing that half-defiant, half-vulnerable look that small boys specialise in. 'Mora,' he muttered, 'I got lost.'

'I'll give you got lost, my lad,' Adam told him with a severity that fooled no one. 'Just look at all these people you've had searching for you!'

Richie turned his wide grey eyes from one to the other of them curiously, then looked back at Adam. 'I'm sorry,' he said simply. 'I didn't *mean* to get lost.'

'No doubt,' Adam said dryly, 'but you did, and now I've had to carry you all the way back from the loch like a babe in arms. Aren't you ashamed of yourself?'

For a moment the two faces, so uncannily alike, looked at each other in silence, then Richie nodded briefly. 'I can stand up,' he announced firmly. 'I'm not hurt, Adam.'

Without a word Adam stood him on his feet, a small stocky figure of independence in the centre of the group of curious faces, with Adam's jacket still draped round him and long enough to reach to his ankles. Mora felt an almost irresistible desire to giggle at the sight he presented and she felt sure that, for a moment, a glimmer of amusement shone in Sir James fierce blue eyes.

'Now that all the fuss is over,' Sir James said in his hearty voice, 'I'll get back to the fire.' He stood, stiffly erect, for a moment, his broad face looking oddly embarrassed and uncertain. 'You'd better come too, Adam,' he added, awkwardly hearty and cheerful. 'Bring the boy with you.'

For a moment Adam stared his surprise, then the familiar glitter of mockery swept over them all and he

151

shook his head. 'No, thanks, Father, we'll go back to the cottage. Richie needs cleaning up, *and* feeding, I don't doubt. We'll manage.'

Mora was as much dismayed at the tone of the refusal as by the refusal itself. It could have been at no small cost to his pride that Sir James had offered the truce and Adam, she felt, should have made the most of his opportunities. Knowing Adam, however, she realised that it was no more than she should have expected of him. He too had his pride and it would take more than an impulsive gesture on the part of his father to appease it.

'Are we going home?' Richie demanded, tugging at Adam's hand.

'Right now,' Adam agreed. He raised his eyes, meeting his father's bright blue gaze steadily. 'I'm grateful to you all for coming out to help,' he said quietly. 'Thank you.' Sir James, Mora thought, would have repeated his invitation—even at the risk of a further snub, but Adam gave him no time to voice it. 'Come on, Richie,' he told the boy, 'let's go and get you cleaned up.'

CHAPTER ELEVEN

WITH the contrariness of February weather, the following day was without rain and the sun even made a short but wan effort to appear. Mora had been thinking about Richie ever since she had watched him go off with Adam the day before; the two dark heads, so much alike, the same jaunty arrogance in their walk as they went towards Adam's cottage.

No one had mentioned the boy again, except Tizzy when they arrived back, but Mora was sure that Sir James' impulsive invitation to Adam had stirred more than one conscience, at least she fervently hoped so. A truce between Adam and his family was long overdue, she felt, and after today and Adam's blunt refusal to bring the boy back to the castle, she wondered if he might not be as much to blame for the continued hostility as anyone. He was stubborn and cursed with as much obstinate pride as the rest of his family, with that persistent streak of devilishness letting him find the situation amusing.

She would, she decided early on in the day, walk down to Effie Smith's cottage some time during the day and make sure that the boy was none the worse for his experience. Her good intentions, however, were frustrated by an unexpectedly large amount of work for Sir James and it was late afternoon before she had the opportunity. By then it was much too dark to venture down the muddy path alone and anyway, there was scarcely time before dinner. It would have to wait until tomorrow.

She had just left the dining room after dinner when she saw Adam coming from the study, and he flicked her a smile to which she found it hard not to respond. He showed none of the taut anxiety of yesterday, but seemed fully restored to his usual slightly cynical good humour. The deep grey eyes swept over her appraisingly, approving the pale pink dress she wore which enhanced the glow in her cheeks and complemented the shiny dark curls, softly awry over her forehead.

'Festivities over?' he enquired, the familiar mockery arousing only a faint prickle of resentment.

'We've finished dinner,' she agreed.

'And now you're free for the evening?' she raised her eyes curiously, wondering what, if anything, lay behind the question.

'As far as I know,' she admitted cautiously. 'I did say I may play canasta with Hamish and the others later on, but——' She stopped, conscious of his amused gaze, her cheeks flushing when she realised that she had been ready to abandon her plans if he should offer an alternative arrangement. 'I had intended going along to see how Richie was, some time today,' she told him stiffly, 'but I've had no chance, we've been rather busy. How is he?'

'He's fine,' he said, taking up the familiar stance as if he was in no hurry to leave. 'He's staying with me for a day or two. Poor Effie was in a bit of a state after he went off like that; apparently he has a habit of escaping when he can, and she's always having to fetch him back when the weather's bad.'

Mora smiled. 'I know,' she said, 'I've brought him back myself several times when he's been down by the burn.'

He looked at her quizzically for a moment. 'Have you?' he said. 'You two are pretty good pals, by the sound of it.'

She looked uneasy, as if her affection for Richie might be interpreted to include himself. 'He's a nice child,' she said. 'Have you got room for him in the cottage?'

'Plenty,' he averred. 'Ramsey and I are playing nurse-maid for a while and we're getting on quite well at the moment.'

'He's not ill?' she asked anxiously, and he shook his head.

'Not a bit,' he said. 'He can run rings round poor old Ramsey, so you have no need to worry about him. He's just staying with us to give Effie Smith a chance to draw breath. He's a bit of a handful, you know.'

'So I believe. Can you cope?' Her eyes danced mischief at the thought, despite her attempt to be serious. 'I mean, two men with a child.'

'Of course we can.' The deep grey eyes swept over her face thoughtfully. 'Of course it does *need* a woman's touch really, but he's been fed and washed and he seems to have no complaints. Ramsey said he'd put him to bed, so I took it he knew what he was doing.'

'And left him to it?' she chided. 'That was cowardly of you.'

'Wasn't it though?' he agreed with a grin. 'Don't you worry about Richie, he's all right.'

'I sincerely hope so,' Mora said feelingly. 'It seems rather a precarious fate, to me, being left in the care of two inexperienced bachelors.'

The arrogant gaze surveyed her for a moment. 'Are you any more experienced in child care?' he retorted. 'Anyway, you can come across and reassure yourself if you like.' There was a glint of challenge in his eyes when he made the suggestion and he did not miss the hasty glance she gave at the closed door of the dining room. 'Unless, of course, you think Hamish would object,' he added softly.

Her blue eyes sparkled defiance at any objection Hamish, or anyone else, might have and she put a foot on the first step of the stairs, her gaze going unerringly to the painted image of the first Adam McLean. 'I'll come,' she said shortly, 'just to see that Richie's all right, but I'll need to fetch a coat first.'

'I'll wait.' He smiled as if the answer had been only what he expected and for a moment she was sorely tempted to change her mind, just to show him that he was not always right.

It was only minutes later that she rejoined him in the hall and he smiled his approval of the soft fur that framed her face and fitted snugly round her neck. 'You look very beautiful,' he said softly, and she flushed at the disturbing intensity of his gaze as he stood for a moment just looking at her.

'Perhaps I should tell someone I'm going,' she ventured, to cover her uneasiness.

He shook his head, a wry smile tilting his straight mouth as he took her arm and they walked across the hall to the door. 'There's no need,' he informed her blithely. 'Hamish put in an appearance while you'd gone for your coat and I told him you were visiting Richie. He wasn't very pleased, but there wasn't much he could do about it short of starting an argument and making a fool of himself.' The sheer arrogance of the statement angered her so that she pulled her arm free of his grasp and went down the steps, stiffly independent.

'Hamish has more sense than to *want* to start an argument about it,' she told him. 'He knows I'm fond of Richie—and I wish you wouldn't always be so patronising towards him.'

'Hamish? I didn't know I was.' He sounded genuinely surprised, and she had no way of judging his expression, for it was dark outside and only the diffused light from the tall windows lit their way along the front of the castle to the rear archway.

She allowed him to take her arm again as they crossed the cobbled stable yard at the back, for the uneven surface of the stones was dangerous in the dark. The silent dampness of grass deadened their footsteps after a few yards when they struck off at an angle towards the stone cottage which he now shared with Ramsey and Richie. They were near the corner of the vast barn-like building that served as garage room for the family's cars, when he drew her to a halt in the

156

shelter of the stone wall and looked down at her in the yellow light of a corner lamp on the building.

'Adam——' She did not know what her protest was to be or even why she should make it, but the wild, uneasy pulse in her temple was throbbing a warning and she knew he must be aware of it, for he held her hands between his own.

'I'm sorry I was—what you choose to call patronising, about Hamish,' he said, and she could hardly restrain a smile at the droll face he presented. 'And I'm sorry I didn't thank you properly for coming out to look for Richie yesterday.'

She shook her head, meeting his eyes only briefly before lowering her own. 'You thanked us all,' she reminded him. 'And you don't have to apologise for anything yesterday—I understood how you felt.'

'I knew you would,' he said, 'but I wanted to make my peace with you.'

'Why?' she asked, genuinely curious. 'Is it important?'

'*I* think so.' He still held her hands tightly between his own. 'You're not sorry you persuaded me to stay on at Glen Ghyll, are you?'

She raised startled eyes to look at him, a protest already forming on her lips. 'I *didn't* persuade you to stay,' she objected. 'You can't say that, Adam.'

'I can and I do,' he assured her, his eyes mocking her protest, glittering almost blackly in the yellow light.

'But you said you'd already been thinking about it,' she insisted. 'I didn't persuade you, Adam, you asked me what I thought and I told you—that's all.'

He looked down at her, the solemnity of his voice belied by the expression in his eyes. 'Ah, but you don't realise how persuasive you can be, Paddy.'

He had not used that ridiculous nickname for some time now and for some reason it gave her a feeling of nostalgia for the days when old Ian McLean had been alive. 'Don't call me that,' she said, but without the usual anger in the

157

words that she had always shown before.

'Sorry.' The deep grey eyes made their swift appraisal of her face with an intensity that threatened to shatter her composure. 'You *do* miss Grandfather McLean, don't you?' She looked startled at the accuracy of his guess and he laughed softly as he lifted the hands he held to rest above his heart. 'I haven't called you Paddy since the old man died, have I?' he asked gently.

'I—I don't know, I don't remember.' She wished her heart would not behave so erratically and that she could not feel the steady beat of his under her curled fingers. There was that familiar and dangerous throb of excitement he could always arouse in her and she sought to steady her voice as she spoke as matter-of-factly as she could. 'Shouldn't we go before someone sees us from the windows?' she asked. They were well illuminated by the lamp overhead and it would be easy to identify them from the windows in the castle that faced this way—as Hamish's did.

For a moment he made no move to release her, then laughed shortly and moved away from her. 'Of course,' he said dryly. 'That would never do, would it?' He turned and held out a hand to her. 'Come on, Paddy, come and see how the other half lives.'

It was only a short distance more to the cottage and when Adam opened the door the light flooded over them in welcome, while the dark face of Ramsey turned a benign smile on them. 'The laddie's fast asleep,' he informed Adam. 'His heid had no touched the pillow before he was away.'

Adam smiled his thanks, shrugging off his jacket in the warmth of the small room and taking Mora's coat as she looked around the homely, comfortable room, comparing it with the vast grandeur of the castle apartments. The cottage was bigger than the impression given by a distant view and it had a cosily untidy air about it which she felt stemmed from Adam's occupation rather than from Ramsey's more recent arrival.

158

Adam hung up her coat and turned and looked at her quizzically. 'How do you like my castle?' he asked, and he laughed at her nod of approval. 'But of course you prefer the grand life, don't you?'

'I do no such thing!' she retorted readily. 'I spent several years in a small London flat, so my ideas aren't as grand as you seem to think.'

'Then Hamish rescued you and whisked you off to his castle,' he teased and, but for the watching Ramsey, she would have retaliated with interest as she had always done in old Ian McLean's time—something that both the old man and Ramsey had always enjoyed. She thought Ramsey looked a mite disappointed at her meek acceptance of the taunt, but she was less inclined at the moment to indulge her temper for the sake of amusing Adam McLean.

'If you like,' she agreed, and Adam too looked disappointed. 'Can I see Richie?' she asked, her gaze turning to the half amused, curious features of Ramsey as he stood near the door into the kitchen. 'If you're sure it won't disturb him, of course.'

'Ye'll no disturb *him*,' Ramsey opined with a smile. He turned to Adam. 'Will I make ye an' the young lady some coffee, sir?'

Adam nodded without consulting Mora and the little man disappeared into the small kitchen. 'In here,' Adam told her, opening a door off the sitting room. 'It's not very big, but then neither is Richie and he likes it well enough.'

The bedroom was indeed small, but it was snug and warm and a night light burned on a shelf, above the reach of small hands, the soft glow of it giving just enough light to see by. Adam crossed to the narrow wooden bed where Richie lay, in far too deep a sleep to be disturbed by their lowered voices, and looked down at the sleeping face and tousled head. It was typical of a man's ministrations, Mora thought wryly, that Ramsey had not thought it necessary to use a hair-brush before putting him to bed.

'He looks very peaceful,' she whispered, an unaccountable huskiness in her voice, 'and much younger than usual.'

'He's five next month,' Adam said, perching himself on the edge of the bed, as if the sight of the sleeping child fascinated him. He glanced up at her suddenly, a faint glint of mockery in his eyes. 'You're curious about him, aren't you, Paddy?'

Mora flushed at the directness of the question. 'Not really,' she said. 'I don't consider it concerns me in fact, does it?'

He looked at her for a long moment, the soft yellow light etching dark, expressive lines about his mouth and eyes. 'Doesn't it?' he asked. 'Don't you want to know who he is?' She shook her head uncertainly and he smiled. 'Oh, come *on*, Paddy, aren't you in the least bit curious?'

It seemed he was bent on teasing her into admitting her curiosity, and she wished she could stop the mad racing of her heart at the prospect of being told by Adam himself that the boy was his son. It was something she had prayed she would never have to hear.

She drew a deep breath and looked down at her twined fingers. 'I—I know he's your son,' she whispered. 'Hamish told me.'

He did not reply at once, but his smile had a curious pathos about it, lacking its usual mockery. 'Yes, he would,' he said quietly, at last. 'It would be too much for him to resist in the circumstances.' His eyes held hers for a long moment, deep and fathomless, and she felt the familiar rapid throb of the pulse in her temple. 'Do you believe it?' he asked, and something in his voice sent her thoughts whirling busily round all sorts of possibilities.

'I—I don't know, Adam.' She wished he had not asked her so forthrightly, but it was typical of him that he had. She looked at the face of the sleeping boy; at the thick dark hair and square chin. Closed lids and a sweep of dark lashes now concealing the grey eyes, so like those of the man who watched her silently. 'He's very like you.' He made no comment still, only watched her patiently. 'And—and there

160

is a special sort of rapport between you. I've noticed it each time I've seen you together.' She struggled with words that could hurt terribly if she used them wrongly. 'I think he *could* be, but it's—it's not like you to deny him if he is.'

He made no immediate answer; looking down at the smaller replica of his own features, one gentle hand brushing back the hair from the boy's forehead. 'Thank you,' he said simply—and she knew that Hamish was wrong.

'But who——?' she began, and he looked up at her and smiled.

'If you'd like to know, I'll tell you,' he said. 'There's only Ramsey knows the truth about the boy now that Grandfather is dead.'

She looked startled for a moment. 'You mean that even——?'

'Even?' His brows arched at her queryingly and she shook her head.

'It doesn't matter,' she said hastily. 'I just wondered as you were so close——'

'Oh, I see,' he laughed shortly. 'No, even Helen doesn't know.' As usual he had guessed what was in her mind and for a second a trace of the more usual devil-may-care light glinted in his eyes as he looked at her. 'You jump to too many conclusions, Paddy. You shouldn't, you know, it's one of the less desirable family traits. Anyway,' he added more soberly, 'Helen doesn't like children, and especially Richie.'

Mora nodded, imagining what Helen Murdoe's feelings must have been when the man who had refused to marry her came home with a boy who was presumably his son by another woman. It must have been a bitter pill to swallow and had probably only been made palatable by the thought of Adam eventually inheriting Glen Ghyll when Sir James died. Adam had been insistent that Helen was more interested in Glen Ghyll than in him personally, and Mora thought it was probably quite true. It would be difficult to imagine the hard determination of the other girl being softened by love.

'I can understand how she feels,' Mora said, and he looked surprised.

'Can you?' he asked, the familiar glint of challenge setting her heart racing again so that she shook her head instinctively, half turning away from him.

'Who *is* Richie?' she asked, seeking some safer subject than her own uncertain feelings.

He sobered again as he looked down at the boy. 'Who is Richie?' he repeated softly. 'My father has another sister besides Aunt Alison, you know. Margaret—she lives in Australia. She went out there over twenty years ago and married an Australian named John Mellors. My cousin, Ann, was born out there and until four years ago I'd never seen her. To be brief, she was indiscreet enough to fall in love with one of the station hands who worked for her father, and when her lover—if you can call him that—discovered how things were, he took off and left her.'

'Poor girl!' It was an all too familiar story, but it would be no less heartbreaking for the girl concerned, Mora thought.

'John Mellors isn't a forgiving type of man, I discovered.' His straight mouth twisted bitterly for a moment. 'It's a trait he shares with *our* family. Anyway, he sent Ann packing when he found out and she had to cope with things as best she could, both before and after Richie was born. She was using the name Gordon when I found her and dying of some horrible illness brought on by neglect. That was nearly four years ago now—Richie was in a children's home.'

'Poor little soul!' She knew the words were inadequate, but he sensed her sympathy and nodded.

'It was a dreadful place to put children. He was only a baby then, of course, but so quiet and subdued, you'd never know him for the same child now. It was so——' He spread his hands in a gesture of hopelessness that seemed so alien to him. 'Ann died within three weeks of my finding her and I got her permission to take Richie away from that place.

162

We travelled around a bit and it was rough on him some-times, but at least he had some sort of chance, and we managed.'

'You managed on your own, with a baby?' She stared at him wide-eyed with surprise and he smiled briefly, shaking his head.

'Not strictly speaking on my own,' he admitted. 'I wasn't exactly roughing it on nothing a day, and he had a succes-sion of nurses and housekeepers. One way and another we coped quite well, I think.' Mora shook her head in be-wilderment. 'Then,' Adam went on, 'when I came back here. I brought him with me.'

Mora stared at him, her eyes wide with disbelief. 'You mean that even after your cousin died, Richie's grand-parents didn't want him?'

He shrugged, bitterness etching deeply into his dark face, something she had never seen before. 'I think Aunt Mar-garet may have relented, but John Mellors is a hard man. I couldn't put Richie into a home again, so when I came home about two years ago, I brought him here. Effie Smith has him most of the time because I have to leave him.'

Mora swallowed hard on the tears that threatened and looked down at the peaceful face of Richie. 'And you let everyone think he was your son,' she said. 'Why, Adam?'

The old familiar look of challenge appeared and he laughed softly. 'Because they took one look at him and assumed the worst from their point of view,' he said, his eyes glittering defiance. 'I was already branded as the black sheep over the business of Helen, so I didn't bother argu-ing. Besides,' his eyes glittered at her wickedly in the soft light, 'I'm quite proud of my son.'

For a moment doubt clouded Mora's eyes and she looked at him steadily. 'Adam, he *isn't* your son, is he?'

He smiled the same challenging smile as always. 'Would it make any difference if he was?' he asked, and she shook her head, sure at last that it did not.

'No, of course it wouldn't. I like Richie, it doesn't matter to me who his father is. I like him.'

'And what about me?' he asked softly. 'Does not being Richie's father improve my status or not?'

She turned away so that the soft yellow light made shadows on her cheeks and turned her dark-fringed eyes to fathomless blue. 'It makes no difference,' she said after a brief, telling silence. 'And you couldn't be a better father to him even if you *were* his real one.'

'Thank you.' He stood up then and took her hands in his, in the same incredibly gentle way he had with Richie. 'I told you the truth, Mora, he's Ann's boy. I've no idea who his father is, I didn't ask, but fortunately he's inherited old Adam's looks, as I have.' He smiled ruefully. 'Fortunately or unfortunately, it's a debatable point. But I'm fond of him and I couldn't part with him now, not for anyone.'

Mora blinked. 'Would anyone expect you to?' she asked, and he laughed shortly, turning away from the little bed and opening the door into the living room where Ramsey had brought a coffee tray and discreetly withdrawn again to the kitchen.

'I don't know,' he said as she joined him in the doorway. 'Would *you*?'

CHAPTER TWELVE

It was much later than she had intended when Mora returned home, and she could not help smiling at the exaggerated caution Adam displayed when he opened the huge, rather squeaky doors to let her in. He could, she thought, give even the most commonplace happening an air of adventure, and his grin of delight at the apparently deserted lower floor reminded her of Richie.

'They're all in bed,' he informed her knowingly, and added with a wicked grin, 'but I know one at least who won't be sleeping until you're safely back in the fold.' Her frown should have quelled him, but she doubted if it would and she shook her head discouragingly.

'Goodnight,' she said softly, almost afraid to break the silence that enveloped them.

'Goodnight.' He bent his head and for a moment she felt the warmth of his lips on her own. 'Be good.' He left her before she could think of a suitable reply, an admonishing finger to his lips.

She closed the big doors carefully and turned to see a tiny glimmer of light below the door of the big room. Curiously she crossed the hall and opened the door. Hamish stood before the remains of the fire in a posture reminiscent of Adam, and more aggressive than his usual stance so that she felt a momentary prickle of warning as she looked at him.

He raised his eyes when she came into the room, then drained the glass he held, with great deliberation, before he spoke. 'I was beginning to think you'd changed your quarters,' he said tartly, and Mora flushed at the implication.

'I'm sorry I'm a bit late, Hamish.' She tried to keep her feelings from her voice. 'We were talking and the time seemed to go so quickly.'

'Talking?' He arched his dark brows in disbelief, then put down the glass with studied care before looking at her again.

Mora felt her temper rise as it usually did only with Adam. 'Yes, talking,' she insisted. 'And if you're worried about my reputation, Ramsey was there too, and the cottage is too small for the kind of goings on that you're hinting at.'

For a moment she thought he would deny that any such thing had entered his head, but his every word since she had come in had been an accusation and he was too honest to deny it. 'I'm sorry, Mora, I should have known you better.'

She crossed the room and stood before him, a wry smile touching her mouth as she raised her eyes and looked at him. 'There are quite a lot of people you should know better, Hamish, but jumping to conclusions is a family trait, isn't it?'

For a moment he made no reply, merely looking down at her in a way that was half curious, half understanding. 'You're referring to Adam, of course,' he said. 'But I don't quite see in what connection.'

She stifled a yawn behind one hand. 'Let's leave it for tonight, shall we?' she said. 'I'm very tired and I'm sure you are.' She tip-toed and kissed him beside his mouth, gently. 'Goodnight, Hamish, and thank you for waiting up for me.'

'Mora!' He put both hands on her arms and pulled her closer to him, his eyes dark in the overhead light, and then, before she quite realised his intention, he kissed her, long and hard so that she fought for breath, more angry with him than she would have thought possible.

'Hamish, stop it!'

For a moment he looked at her in surprise. She had objected to being kissed in that way before, but never so

166

vehemently, and he frowned over what he took to be the reason. 'Adam,' he said accusingly, and she shook her head firmly, determined not to discuss any of it tonight.

'I'm tired,' she repeated. 'I don't want to get involved with anything else tonight, Hamish. Goodnight.' He would have argued, she felt, but her expression was determined enough to quell his argument and she moved away from him towards the door, turning to smile at him over her shoulder. 'Goodnight, Hamish,' she repeated softly, and closed the door gently behind her.

In contrast to the previous day, there was almost nothing for her to do on the Tuesday and, since the day was fine and promised well, she decided to ride out as far as Glencairn. Mist was more than eager to comply and welcomed the opportunity of more exercise than a mere trot around the stable yard offered.

The road was still patterned with numerous puddles, like outsize pennies in their path, but it was fine enough to make the ride pleasant and she enjoyed the feel of the wind briskly whipping a glow into her cheeks when she put Mist into a trot.

She left the road before she reached the village, turning along the path that skirted the loch, a path she had not used since she had fallen into the snowdrift and been rescued by Adam. It was muddy underfoot, but the going was firm enough to suit Mist and he plodded along at his own tranquil pace, leaving Mora to sort out her rather confused thoughts.

She had tried in vain to persuade Adam to tell his family the truth about Richie, but he had been adamant, only laughing when she threatened to do so herself if he did not change his mind. His laughter had given her the idea that perhaps he would not be averse to her acting as peacemaker between him and his family, and it was this thought that so preoccupied her as she rode round the loch.

How she would tell Sir James and the others that they

had made a terrible mistake about Richie, she had no idea, but the urge to tell them was so strong that she had thought of nothing else since last night and she felt she could not hold her tongue for much longer. Of course, Adam was far from blameless, for he should have told them the truth right from the beginning—but being Adam she could see that it would not have been in character for him to have done so.

So busy was she with her thoughts that she was not aware of Helen Murdoe until the other girl reined in in front of her, a smile on her face at Mora's start of surprise. 'Are you not working this morning, Miss O'Connell?' she asked in her soft voice, the dark eyes as usual appraising Mora's wind-flushed cheeks and preoccupied expression.

'Not at the moment,' Mora replied. 'We were very busy yesterday. I think Sir James is taking it easy today.'

She resented the girl's curiosity and the insinuation in her words that implied she should not have been out riding but hard at work and earning her pay.

'It seems to me that Sir James is a very indulgent employer,' Helen Murdoe opined. 'I'd not pay anyone good money to go riding around the country like a lady of leisure.'

Mora felt the anger rise in her despite her efforts to take a reasonable view of the girl's acid tongue. Her eyes sparkled brightly with it as she gripped the rein tightly to control her temper. 'Sir James *is* a very considerate employer,' she agreed. 'As a matter of fact it was his suggestion that I should come out riding this morning.' If that was not strictly true, at least Sir James had smiled approval when she had announced her intention of coming, and approval was encouragement, Mora felt.

'You're alone, I see.' The beautiful eyes, she thought, held a gleam of satisfaction. 'Is Hamish too busy to be with you these days?'

'Not always,' Mora said. 'But he was today. Besides,' she added honestly, 'I like riding alone.'

There was not only doubt but frank disbelief in the gaze that greeted that statement, and the girl's rather thin lips curled derisively. 'It's as well since you've no one to ride with,' she said.

Try as she would, Mora could not disguise the dislike she felt for Helen Murdoe and she suspected that the other girl knew it. Her temper was rapidly getting the better of her as she met the taunting gleam in the wide dark eyes. 'You appear to like your own company too, I see,' she said, quietly polite still.

A smile as malicious as a cat's revealed Helen Murdoe's white, even teeth. 'But I haven't been alone,' she said in her soft voice. 'Adam was with me until a few minutes ago.'

For some reason Mora felt that this was the last thing she had wanted to hear, although she should have known, she told herself. Whatever Adam said, there *was* something between him and Helen Murdoe, she felt sure, and she found the thought far more dismaying than she cared to admit. 'Oh—I see,' she said, noncommittally, she hoped.

'I'm sure you do,' Helen Murdoe said softly, and with such malice that Mora felt a shiver tremble along her spine, her fingers tightening on the rein.

'If you'll excuse me, Miss Murdoe,' Mora said stiffly, 'I'll get on. The wind is chill if one stands around too long.'

Again a smile of satisfaction spread slowly across the gauntly attractive face. 'You'll not be in time to catch Adam,' she averred. 'He'll be well on his way back by now.'

Subconsciously, Mora supposed, the idea of catching up with Adam had been in her mind, but she fiercely resented the other girl's insinuation and her cheeks flushed brightly pink as she put her heels sharply to a surprised Mist and sent him into a gallop, away from the taunting smile of Helen Murdoe.

She had ridden more than half-way round the loch before

she reined in Mist to a more reasonable pace and the animal shook his head and snorted his disapproval at so much unexpected activity, resorting again to his steady plod as they headed for home.

It was not until she took time to look around her that Mora realised she was not the only rider on the path and she felt a momentary tingle of panic when Adam turned in the saddle and waved a hand to her, almost as if he sensed her approach. He reined in the big black he rode, to wait for her, seemingly content to wait on Mist's easy pace.

It must look, she thought uneasily, as if she had been trying to catch up with him, and she wished she had not galloped her animal quite so long or so hard, but the speed and the sting of the wind had done something to cool her temper and make her feel more rational.

The deep grey eyes swept over her flushed cheeks and windblown hair as she rode up, and might have guessed her mood from the bright glitter in her eyes. She had lost the protection of the scarf covering her hair during the gallop and her dark hair blew freely into a tumble of curls about her face. He said nothing for a moment, but there was a warmth in his gaze which she found disturbing.

'I thought you would have caught me earlier, from the speed you were travelling,' he told her. 'Poor old Mist hasn't moved so fast for years.' He leaned over and patted the neck of her animal, the movement bringing him closer to her, the deep eyes looking at her curiously.

'I hadn't even seen you, actually,' she said hastily. 'I was just anxious to get away from——' She bit her lip on the girl's name, but the precaution was unnecessary. She could tell from his expression that he knew of her meeting with Helen Murdoe.

'From Helen?' he asked, and she did not reply. 'You two just don't like each other, do you?' he added, and looked at her slyly from the corners of his eyes. 'I wonder why.'

'It doesn't matter why,' she said shortly. 'You like her and I don't—let's leave it at that, shall we?'

'I don't know whether I like her or not,' he demurred. 'I've certainly known her a long time; all our lives, in fact.'

She stared at him, a frown of disbelief between her brows. 'But surely if you and she——' Again she bit her lip on what could have been an indiscretion, and he laughed— the soft deep sound that always made her heart jump uneasily.

'If you're referring to the fact that Helen broke off her engagement to Hamish because of me,' he told her blandly, 'that, my dear Paddy, was entirely Helen's idea, not mine.'

'But——' She searched the dark arrogant face for some sign of regret, but found none.

'But you think I should at least show some sign of being ashamed of myself for being the cause of Hamish's—shall we be old-fashioned and call it heartbreak?—is that it?'

'I wasn't going to word it quite like that,' she denied. 'But Hamish must have been fond of her to become engaged to her, surely. And if you were the reason it broke up, I would have thought——'

'I don't really see why I should be sorry about it.' he interrupted, and sent her a wry smile. 'After all, look what happened to him eventually. He met you—and it wouldn't have been so easy for him to lure you back here if he'd been a married man, would it?'

'Of course not,' she said indignantly. 'The situation wouldn't even have arisen. And anyway,' she added, not to be sidetracked, 'it was *your* part in the affair we were talking about, not Hamish's.'

He shrugged. 'As for that—as Hamish and the family saw it, I was a black-hearted villain who seduced his brother's fiancée and then deserted her.' He laughed at her embarrassed expression. 'I'm sorry to use such hackneyed clichés, Paddy, but they fit the situation.'

'If they were wrong why didn't you tell them?' she asked, knowing the answer full well. 'No, of course you wouldn't,' she added before he could reply, and he laughed again.

'They wouldn't have believed me if I had,' he said dryly.

'You didn't give them the chance,' she retorted. 'They might have done.'

'Will you?' he asked, and leaned across and covered her hands with one of his own. 'I'd like you to hear my side of it for a change, Mora, unless you're not interested, of course.'

'Of course I am,' she said hastily. 'I'm sorry, Adam. I misjudged you once on hearsay, I'd hate to do it again.'

He withdrew his hand from hers, needing both to control the big black to the steady pace of Mist. 'Bless you, Paddy. I'll tell you what really happened about Helen, then you can judge for yourself just how much of a villain I am.' He rode on silently for a few seconds, gathering his thoughts she suspected. 'Hamish had always been closer to Helen than any of us,' he said, at last, 'I suppose because they were nearer in age, and they were only eighteen when he proposed to her. It was a foregone conclusion as far as the family were concerned. The McLean men usually marry young so their ages didn't worry them at all. Helen's father was alive then and they were quite well to do, or so everyone thought. Less than six months later Alec Murdoe died and Helen and her mother realised just how little money there really was.' There was nothing but sympathy for the girl and her mother when he spoke and Mora could imagine that his kindness had been his undoing, at least as far as Helen was concerned.

'It must have been an awful shock to them both,' she said, genuinely sorry for the two women.

'It was disastrous as far as Helen was concerned,' he said grimly. 'She was an only child and she'd never wanted for anything without getting it, all her life. The thought of being suddenly—well, less than wealthy, appalled her. Hamish could have made her comfortably off, of course, but that wasn't enough for Helen, I think she actually hated us for a while for being so filthy rich, she wanted it all, and

172

the only way she could make sure of it was to break with Hamish and declare herself in love with me.'

'You didn't—enourage her?' She stared at him wide-eyed, trying to grasp the enormity of Helen Murdoe's blackmail.

He shook his head. 'No. I liked Helen and I sympathised with her, it was an awful position to find herself in after the upbringing she'd had, and I think she panicked when she thought of it. I suppose I seemed the best way out.' He grinned at her wryly. 'I was a ready-made villain, you see, being so much like the old Adam and being—well, fond of feminine company.' He glanced at her to see how she took the last remark, but she feigned not to notice and he went on. 'I didn't see why I should marry her for no better reason than I felt pity for her.'

'And you didn't explain the position to the family at all?'

'I told you they wouldn't have believed me.' He shrugged, uncaringly it seemed. 'Anyway, why should I bother? If they chose to believe the worst of me why should I bother to disillusion them?'

'They believed what Helen told them?'

He nodded. 'I couldn't bring myself to call her bluff, not in the circumstances.' The deep grey eyes smiled at her, asking for understanding, it seemed. 'So I took off, went abroad like the traditional black sheep. I was a coward, I suppose.'

'You weren't!' Her own vehemence surprised her and she saw from his face that he was surprised too. 'But you could have made some explanation to the others. Told them—something.'

'Told them what?' he asked wryly. 'Apart from which I don't believe in explaining myself to all and sundry.'

'And yet you've explained things to me twice in the space of a few hours,' she reminded him softly, but he made no answer for a moment, riding beside her silently, his thoughts busy.

'Almost home,' he said after a moment or two. 'I could tell even if I was blindfold, from the way Klonda starts pulling that way.'

They turned into the stable yard without saying another word and Rob Smith came forward to take the horses, leading them away in his usual dour silence. Mora stood uncertainly for a moment, her way across the yard barred by Adam, who watched her thoughtfully, a faint frown between his brows as if something puzzled him.

'I'd better go and change for lunch,' Mora said, feeling that dizzying throb in her temple again as she made an attempt to pass him.

He still did not speak but put one hand on the wall behind her, the movement bringing him unnervingly close, so that she could see the fringe of thick lashes round the deep grey eyes and the fine lines of laughter at the corners of his mouth. 'Are you going to marry Hamish?' he asked suddenly and unexpectedly, and she shook her head, not trusting herself to speak. 'Does he know?'

'Yes. At least—I've told him, but I'm not sure he believed me.'

'No, he wouldn't.' He was looking down at her with that disturbingly intent gaze fixed on her mouth, so that she was conscious of nothing but the pounding throb of her heart and the nearness of him. She made no protest when his arms went round her, holding her so tightly she could feel his heart beat as well as her own, closing her eyes as his mouth found hers and he kissed her, gently at first and then with growing passion until she clung to him like a drowning child, knowing only that she wanted him never to let her go again.

'Adam.' His name was little more than a sigh of sound when at last she could speak and for a moment he held her close to him, his face resting on the soft tumble of her hair. She raised her face and looked at him, her eyes brighter and deeper blue than they had ever been. 'Adam, let me tell them about—about everything,' she begged.

174

'Why?' he asked, looking down at her with something more behind the usual amused tolerance in his eyes. 'Don't you like being in league with the black sheep?'

'You know I don't care about things like that,' she said reproachfully. 'But in fairness to yourself, Adam, you should tell them about Richie—or let me.'

'Paddy the Peacemaker,' he teased her softly, and planted a kiss beside her mouth. 'Very well, if you feel you must, you can polish up my halo, but for heaven's sake don't make me out to be too much of a saint. It wouldn't suit my image, and old Adam would disown me.'

'I couldn't even if I tried,' she retorted, then sobered suddenly. 'But don't be such a determined villain, Adam,' she pleaded. 'You're not as bad as the original Adam, and I wish you'd stop trying to live up to him.'

The deep grey eyes glittered down at her with all the dark arrogance of the man in the portrait, whose name he bore. 'I have a feeling that history is about to repeat itself yet again,' he told her. 'But I think I shall do rather better than old Adam ever did. Anyway,' he sighed deeply, 'I'm not counting my chickens yet.'

She smiled at him, her eyes bright with mischief. 'I'm sure *he* was never so cautious,' she teased.

'Perhaps not,' he admitted soberly, the dark gaze resting, disturbingly intent, on her mouth. 'But I have more to lose than he ever had.'

'Adam——' she began, but he brushed her lips with his own to silence her.

'Sssh!' he whispered as his mouth came down hard over hers, gentle yet demanding, and she even forgot that she was going to tell him that Hamish had appeared briefly at one of the windows overlooking the yard.

He released her at last and put his hands on her arms to hold her away from him, studying her with such warmth and intensity that she was uncaring whether Hamish or even the whole family saw them. 'I'd better have a talk with Hamish,' he said with a glint of the old mocking humour in his eyes as he looked down at her. 'This isn't going to improve your chances of cleaning up my reputation, you know, Paddy. I've a feeling that one of the family at least isn't going to forgive and forget.'

CHAPTER THIRTEEN

LUNCHTIME that day, Mora thought, was as good a time as any to attempt what Adam had termed cleaning up his reputation, but she found that actually bringing the subject round to Adam and Richie was more difficult than she had anticipated. She hesitated to plunge straight into an explanation for fear of the reactions she might arouse, although she felt sure that Sir James, at least, was prepared to meet his eldest son half-way in any move to heal the breach between them. His invitation of Sunday had proved that.

Hamish's absence from lunch did not make things any easier for Mora, for unless he was required at the works in Cairndale, he always joined the family for lunch and she knew, only too well, that he was not in Cairndale. It was that glimpse she had seen of him earlier, at one of the windows, that made her so uneasy, for there was no doubt in her mind that he would have seen Adam with her by the stables and she felt not a little guilty about it. Hamish would find it hard to believe that her reason for refusing to marry him had been other than a secret love for his brother and he would find her apparent deception unforgivable. She sighed inwardly, as she stirred sugar into her coffee, her expression thoughtful.

'You're very preoccupied, Mora.' Sir James' voice broke into her thoughts and she started, smiling apologetically.

'I'm sorry, Sir James, I was deep in thought.'

'Worrying about something, judging by your expression,' Sir James said. 'Were you, my dear?'

Mora smiled, shaking her head slowly. 'Not really worry-

177

ing,' she demurred. 'But I was wondering why Hamish hadn't joined us for lunch, he usually does when he's here.'

The shrewd blue eyes narrowed briefly as he looked at her. 'He said he wanted to see Adam about something,' Sir James said. 'He didn't say what, but he seemed to me to be thoroughly out of temper—probably he and Adam have had a difference of opinion over something.'

Mora felt the colour flush into her cheeks and was aware of Alison McLean's eyes watching her curiously. 'I—I think I may have—I mean it could concern me,' Mora admitted unhappily, and shook her head when Sir James looked mildly surprised. 'I'm sorry, Sir James, if I've been the cause of even more ill-feeling between Adam and Hamish, but I'm afraid I may have been.'

Sir James nodded slowly. 'I rather thought things had taken a turn in that direction,' he said. 'I'm sorry about it, Mora. Hamish is a good man, and he's been hurt once already in this way.'

'I know,' Mora said softly and with genuine regret. 'And I'm sorry about it too, Sir James, but I told Hamish right from the start that I wasn't in love with him. I wasn't sure of my own feelings at first and I told him that too, but when I was sure that I would never feel any differently I was quite honest about it. I only came here to Glen Ghyll with him on the understanding that he wouldn't take it as an admission of love on my part. He knew that and he accepted it.'

Sir James looked thoughtful. 'I see,' he said slowly. 'So that story about you coming here for research into the McLean history wasn't just a story?'

'Indeed no.' Mora was adamant. 'I admit that Hamish did tell me that he hoped being here with him would change my mind, but it didn't. I've told him several times that I can't marry him. That was the reason I wanted to leave just after Mr. Ian McLean died and when my research was finished.'

'And I persuaded you to stay on.' The shrewd blue eyes

178

studied her for a moment curiously. 'Or was it me that persuaded you? When did you get—involved with Adam?'

She hesitated, unsure at the moment just how involved she was with Adam. He had made no declaration of love as Hamish had done, but there was no doubt about the warmth and sincerity of his kisses or the expression in his eyes when he looked at her. About her own feelings she had no doubt at all. The idea of leaving Glen Ghyll and never seeing Adam again did not bear thinking about.

She spoke slowly when she answered Sir James, choosing her words carefully. 'I think Hamish saw Adam kissing me this morning,' she said. 'I saw him at one of the windows, but it was too late by then.'

'You'd been found out,' Sir James remarked tartly.

'Not found out,' Mora protested. 'I didn't know myself it was going to happen and I had no wish at all for Hamish to witness what he did. I would have told him myself, as soon as I could. There's been nothing underhand either on my part or Adam's, please believe that, Sir James.'

For a moment there was silence in the room, then Sir James leaned across and covered her hand with his own, his blue eyes kindly and apologetic. 'I'm sorry, Mora my dear, I should have known you wouldn't treat Hamish so badly, by going behind his back. But'—he shrugged—'Adam has a reputation for that kind of thing.'

'Do you know about the boy?' It was Alison McLean's brusque and not altogether approving voice that broke in, and Móra looked across at her, briefly startled by the mention of the subject she had been seeking to raise herself.

'I know that you all think Richie is Adam's son,' she said quietly.

Sir James fixed her with his fierce blue eyes, a frown of uncertainty between his brows. 'You say we all *think* the boy is Adam's son. There's no doubt, surely?' There was an echo of hope in the hearty voice, Mora felt sure, but she wondered how this bluff, outspoken man would feel when he learned that for two years he had misjudged his son on no more than the false evidence of his own eyes.

'Of course there's no doubt,' Alison McLean said brusquely. 'That boy is exactly like Adam was at that age.'

Mora's eyes sparkled defiance at the argument. 'Adam is exactly like that painting of his namesake that hangs on the stairs,' she said, 'and Hamish and Fergus aren't. Does that mean that Adam had a different father?'

'Of course not!' Miss McLean looked scandalised. 'And I find it difficult to see a reason for your making such a suggestion, Mora.'

'I think perhaps I *do* see her reason,' Sir James said slowly, his shrewd eyes watching Mora closely. 'Those looks that Adam has inherited don't favour me at all, but I passed them on to him. It's a very distinctive appearance and it hasn't been repeated since my great-grandfather, though he didn't bear quite such a startling resemblance to the portrait as Adam does. I can see the point of your argument, Mora.' He raised enquiring brows. 'But if he isn't Adam's son, who *is* the boy?'

Mora hesitated to inflict still further discomfiting truths on them, but there was no other way to clear Adam. 'You have another sister in Australia, haven't you, Sir James?'

'Yes—Margaret.' Realisation began to dawn on the broad face when Mora nodded. 'You mean——?'

'Richie is Mrs. Mellors' grandson,' Mora told him. 'Adam's his second cousin, not his father.'

'Then what in heaven's name is he doing here with Adam?'

An audible sigh from Alison McLean answered him and Mora looked across at the painful understanding in the older woman's eyes as she carefully folded her table napkin and laid it beside her coffee cup. 'I think I understand,' she said at last quietly, and looked down the length of the table at her brother. 'You remember that rather puzzling letter we received from Margaret some years ago, James? She said that Ann and her father had quarrelled bitterly about something and that Ann had left home. She didn't expect

180

they would ever see her again and we've never heard anything of her since.'

'I do remember,' Sir James said thoughtfully, and turned to Mora. 'Is that right, Mora? *Is* Richie Ann's boy?'

Mora nodded. 'Your niece died four years ago, Sir James,' she said gently. 'Just after Adam found her. Richie was just a baby and in a children's home.'

'And no one said a word to us about it,' Sir James murmured, his blue eyes dark with hurt as he exchanged glances with his sister. 'Margaret might have told us.'

'Perhaps she found it difficult to admit that she couldn't take her grandson and look after him,' Mora suggested. 'Mrs. Mellors would have taken Richie, so Adam said, but her husband wouldn't hear of it, even after Ann died. She wasn't married to Richie's father, you see.'

'I see.' Sir James looked older suddenly and some of the fire seemed to have died in the fierce blue eyes. It was as if he realised that he could not condemn his sister's husband without condemning himself, for their reactions, to a certain extent, had been the same. 'And Adam's had the boy all this time?'

'Ever since his mother died,' Mora agreed softly, feeling intensely sorry for both Sir James and his sister for having their shortcomings so sharply brought home to them by the actions of another. She explained the situation as Adam had explained it to her, but giving Adam rather more credit than he had given himself, and her audience listened attentively and in silence.

'It was those looks,' Sir James said thoughtfully as Mora finished. 'They are so uncannily alike, Adam and the boy, that I thought it impossible that anyone else could have fathered that child.' His eyes narrowed as he looked at Mora. 'Adam should have told us when he first came back,' he said.

Mora met his eyes steadily. 'Was he given the opportunity?' she asked gently.

Sir James held her gaze for a moment, then he shook his

181

head slowly. 'No,' he admitted, 'I suppose not. It was all too easy to jump to the wrong conclusion and Adam was never a man to explain his actions to anyone.' He drew a deep breath, his chin set firm as he folded his hands on the table before him. 'I have to eat humble pie,' he said. 'It won't be easy, but I shall do it because I owe it to Adam.' He shifted his gaze to his sister. 'We all shall,' he decreed.

'Of course,' Alison agreed, and added with a softness that won Mora's heart, 'I hope Adam deals more kindly with us than we did with him.'

Mora reached across and covered the folded hands, her eyes bright and softly shining. 'He will,' she promised.

'It seems,' Sir James said slowly, his eyes on Mora's shining eyes, 'that for a man not given to explaining himself, Adam has been very frank with you, my dear. Is there any special reason for that?'

'I don't know,' Mora confessed, her cheeks flushed under his scrutiny. 'I've learned a lot about Adam in the last few days. I thought you should know about Richie, so I asked Adam to let me tell you.'

'And he agreed?'

Mora nodded. 'Not very graciously, I may add,' she said with a wry smile. 'But I felt you should know in fairness to you as well as Adam. That's why I told you.'

'I'm glad you have,' said Sir James. 'Thank you, my dear.'

Crossing the hall on the way to her room after lunch, Mora turned, momentarily startled, when Hamish called to her from the doorway of the study. 'If you can spare me a moment, Mora, I'd like to talk to you.'

She halted, disturbed by the harsh brusqueness of his voice which made the request almost a command—noting, too, his dishevelled hair and the dark, angry look in his eyes. 'I can spare the time now,' she told him, changing direction and joining him in the study.

Hamish stood by the window, his back half turned to her, as if he did not want her to see the depth of his anger. 'I've seen Adam,' he said abruptly, and waited, apparently for her to comment.

'Have you?' She refused to become flustered or to feel guilty, although it was difficult avoiding the latter when she remembered her own behaviour earlier and the way she had surrendered rather than objected to Adam kissing her.

He turned then and looked down at her. 'I went down and saw him because of what I saw from my bedroom window this morning,' he said, his voice harsh as he fought to control his temper. 'Haven't you anything to say by way of explanation, Mora?'

She flushed at the accusation in his voice and his eyes. 'I don't see that I have anything to explain, Hamish,' she said quietly. 'I admit Adam kissed me, but I don't see that that requires an explanation. I'm a free agent and so is Adam, so there is nothing *to* explain.'

'You don't care about that boy of his?' His lip curled scornfully as if he held her in as low opinion as he did his brother.

'He's not Adam's boy, Hamish!' She flashed her temper at him at last, unable to control it any longer. 'At least he's not his son.' Hamish stared at her in disbelief, doubting every word she said. 'I've just told your father and Miss McLean about Richie,' she said more quietly. 'Richie is your cousin Ann's child, Hamish, not Adam's.'

'You believe that? Because he told you?'

She stared at him wide-eyed, controlling her own explosive temper with difficulty. 'Of course I believe him,' she said. 'It's something Adam wouldn't lie about. I know he wouldn't.'

He held her gaze for a moment, then, when hers did not waver, turned his back on her again, one hand on the frame of the window, his forehead resting briefly against his arm. 'No, he wouldn't,' he agreed reluctantly at last. 'Especially that way.'

'That way?' Mora looked puzzled.

'Saying he *wasn't* his son,' he explained, turning a wry

smile on her. 'He'd be more likely to claim him than disown him; it would be more in keeping with his precious idol in that wretched portrait.' Mora merely nodded agreement and he turned to face her again, taking her hands and holding them tightly under his own, his eyes searching hopefully over her face. 'Mora.'

'Please, Hamish.' She tried to free her hands, hating to look at him when she knew what it was he was going to say.

'I love you, Mora.' He could look incredibly like Adam, she thought dizzily, as he looked down at her, the grey eyes fierce and determined. 'And I'm damned if Adam is going to have you,' he added grimly. 'He took Helen from me, but you're mine. I brought you here and I'm going to marry you.'

'No, Hamish!' She struggled to free her hands. 'And you're wrong about that too. Adam didn't take Helen from you.'

He looked at her for a moment, temporarily distracted, then he shook his head. 'I don't care about Helen now,' he insisted. 'It's you. I want to marry you.'

'Please!' She managed to free her hands at last and stood rubbing her wrists where his fingers had left their mark. 'I've told you, Hamish, I can't marry you because I don't love you. Please understand.'

'But you love Adam?' It was more accusation than statement and for a moment she hesitated, wondering how much or what manner of things Adam had told him, then she lifted her chin, her blue eyes brightly defiant as she looked up at him steadily.

'Yes,' she said clearly, 'I love Adam.'

For a moment he neither moved nor spoke, then he shook his head, standing before her, rather awkwardly, his eyes dark with hurt, a trace of temper still narrowing his straight mouth. 'All right,' he said at last, quietly controlled. 'Go to Adam. I wish you both every happiness.'

'Hamish.' She put out a hand and touched his arm

184

gently, her eyes appealing for understanding. 'I'd like to think you really meant that.'

'I do,' he said with apparent sincerity, then added, 'I hope you fare better than Helen did.'

She shook her head, staring at him in dismay, then without another word, turned and fled from the room. She crossed the hall and would have run straight on up the stairs to her own room, but an arm stopped her headlong flight and brought her to a halt as she reached the first step.

'Mora.' She looked up through the haze of tears that half blinded her and saw Adam's face, his eyes half curious, half sympathetic. 'What's wrong?' he asked.

'Let me go,' she whispered, trying to evade the arm that encircled her waist and held her as if it had no intention of ever letting her go.

'Not until you quieten down,' he said firmly. 'Who upset you? Hamish?' She nodded, miserably uncertain of herself and of him. He sighed. 'Tell me about it,' he said resignedly.

'No, I don't want to talk about it.'

He turned her round to face him. 'Paddy, I shall get really mad with you in a minute,' he warned her. 'If Hamish has upset you, I have a right to know about it, since it probably concerns me, so be a good girl and fetch a coat, then come for a walk with me. Unless,' he added with a glimpse of the old mockery, 'you'd prefer the south tower.'

'So that history can really repeat itself?' she retorted, and he laughed, putting both arms round her and pulling her close so that his chin rested on the top of her head.

'The south tower,' he decreed. 'I'm in a romantic mood, and besides, there's enough wind up there to blow all your cobwebs away.'

She toyed with the idea of refusing for a second or two, then without a word she moved on up the stairs and into her room. Adam followed her as far as the doorway and helped her into the warm coat she took from the wardrobe. 'You'll be cold,' she ventured, seeing him, as usual, without a topcoat and with only a jacket and the customary riding breeches and sweater against the cold wind.

'I'll survive,' he told her with a grin, and put an arm round her shoulders while they walked along the corridor.

It was windy out on the exposed square of the tower, but she found herself unexpectedly warm as they looked down over the wall to the ground below. 'The sun's coming out,' she said hopefully.

He lifted her chin with one finger, seeing her eyes free of tears. 'So I see,' he said softly.

'Adam——'

He kissed her lightly beside her mouth, the deep grey eyes warm and half teasing as he looked down at her. 'I'm glad you love me,' he said, and kissed her mouth before she could protest or deny his assumption. She struggled with reason and curiosity for only a second before the wild, dizzying pulse in her temple blinded her to everything but the strength of his arms and the fierce warmth of his kiss.

'How—how do you know?' she managed at last, held breathlessly tight in his arms while he kissed her neck and throat, burying his face in the softness of her hair.

'How do I know what?' he asked, his voice muffled against her ear.

'That I love you. Adam,' she pulled away from him, just far enough to be able to see his face, her eyes shiningly bright as she studied him, 'how *do* you know?'

He laughed. The soft deep sound that always stirred her pulse. 'You told Hamish,' he said blandly.

'Adam! You were listening!' She frowned her indignation, trying in vain to break his hold on her. 'You had no right.'

'I know,' he admitted blithely. 'But I wasn't actually listening. If you hadn't been so engrossed in your showdown with Hamish, you'd have seen the door of the study open *and* close. I was just in time to hear you proclaim that you loved me and then I closed the door quickly.' He smiled down at her the old glitter of challenge in his eyes.

'After that I felt anything else would have been an anti-climax. It was all I ever wanted to hear.'

She lowered her eyes, the fringe of lashes dark against her cheeks. 'You—you didn't hear what Hamish said?'

'No.' He looked interested. 'What did Hamish say?' She traced the outline of his jacket lapel with one finger, un-answering. 'Mora?' he lifted her chin with one finger. 'Is that what upset you so much?'

'Yes.'

He brushed his lips gently against her forehead. 'Tell me,' he urged.

Mora raised her eyes, uncertainty clouding the shine of happiness in them. 'He said—he said that he hoped I'd fare better than Helen did.'

He was silent for a second, then he hugged her close to him again, his face against her hair, his voice gentle when he spoke. 'Hamish could never resist one last try,' he said. 'But he could have spared you that.'

'I—I didn't really think you'd——' She clung to him for a moment, then raised her face and looked at him.

'I love you,' he told her softly, 'and that's something I've never said to Helen or anyone else. I love you, Mora, and I want to marry you if you'll have me. It's what Grandfather McLean wanted too,' he added with a wry smile that anticipated her look of surprise.

'Did he?' she asked.

He nodded, smiling at her puzzled face. 'He asked you when you were going to marry his grandson, remember?' The light of understanding dawned in her eyes and she nodded. 'He had more than one grandson—but you immediately thought he meant Hamish, didn't you?'

'Yes,' she admitted. 'It was because of what he said when he asked me. He said—"He loves you, I can see it in his eyes"—it never occurred to me that he could mean you.'

'You couldn't believe I was in love with you?' He kissed her gently; on her forehead, her cheeks and the dark-fringed blue eyes. 'Why not, my love?'

'I—I don't know.' She raised her eyes and searched the dark, endearingly familiar face. 'Do you really want to marry me?'

'More than anything in the world,' he assured her. 'But I'll try to understand if you say no. I know I'm not the most reliable man on earth and there *is* Richie to take into account. But please, my love,' the deep grey eyes had a look of appeal she thought must be impossible to resist, 'try not to say no, because I love you so much. Will you marry me?'

The unfamiliar humility brought a shine of tears to her eyes. 'Of course I will,' she said—and the wind round the stone walls of the tower sounded low and soft, like the echo of a man's laugh, as Adam drew her close again and sealed the promise with a kiss.